DISCARD

This book belongs to:

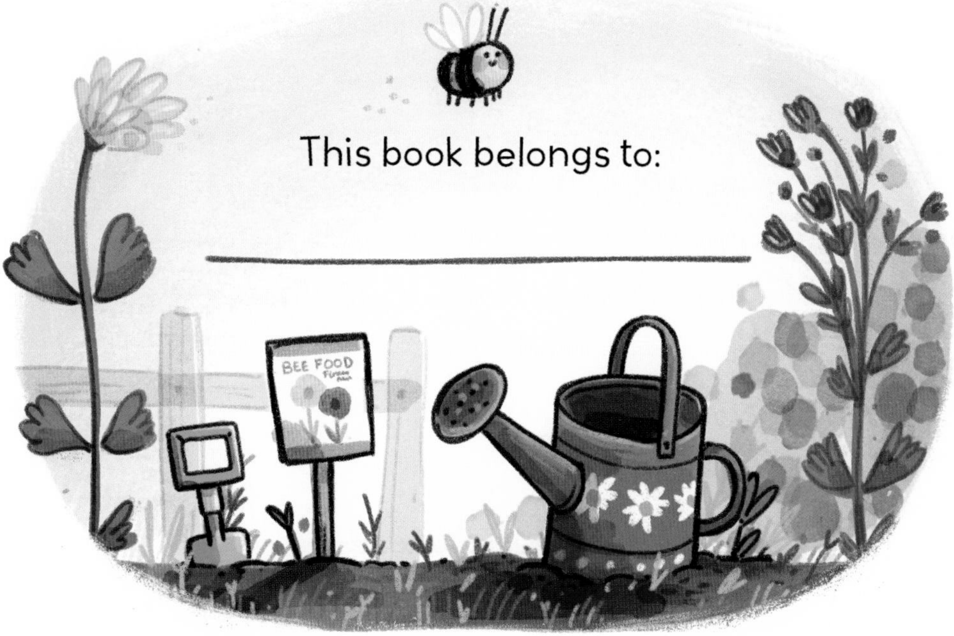
BEE FOOD

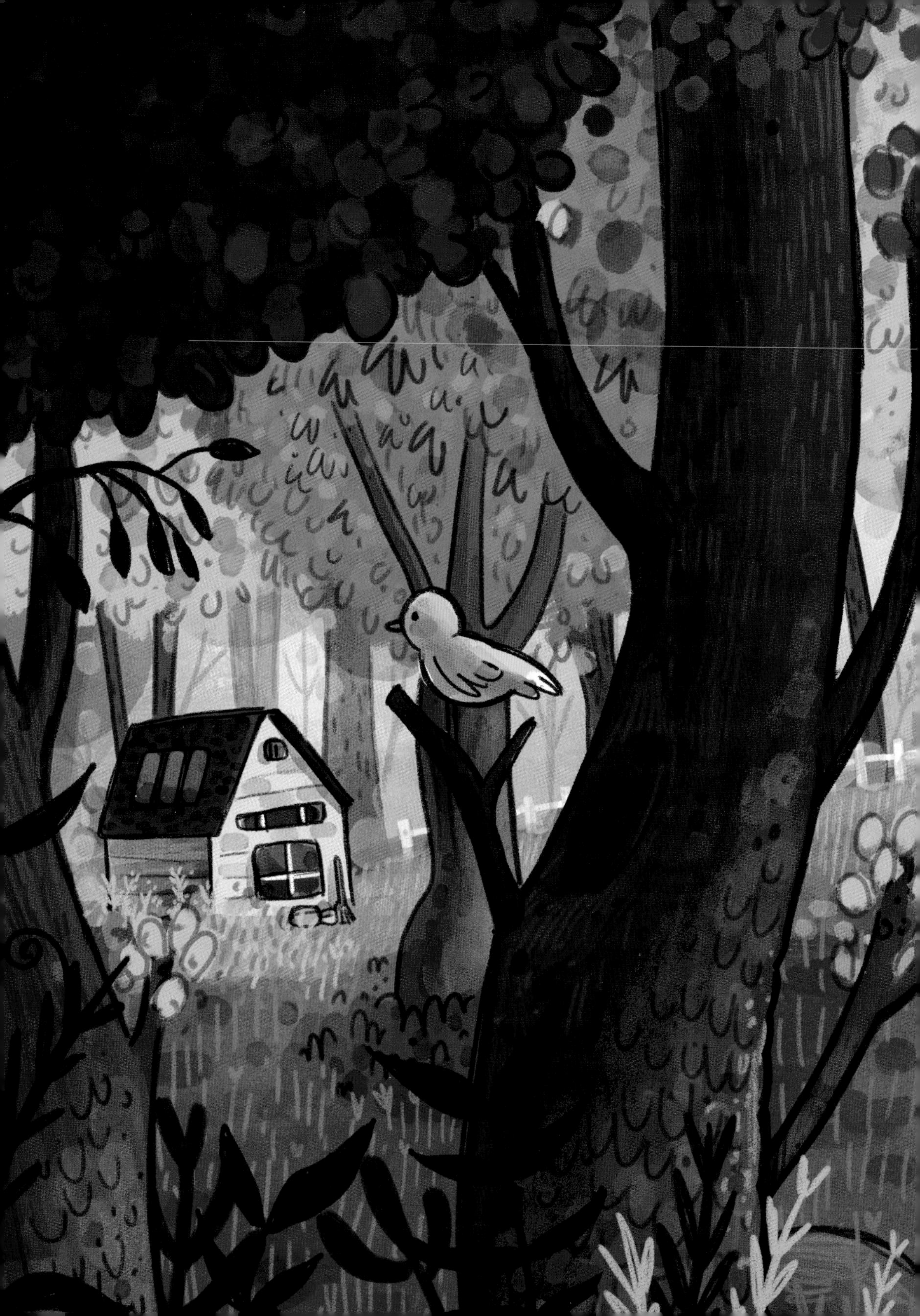

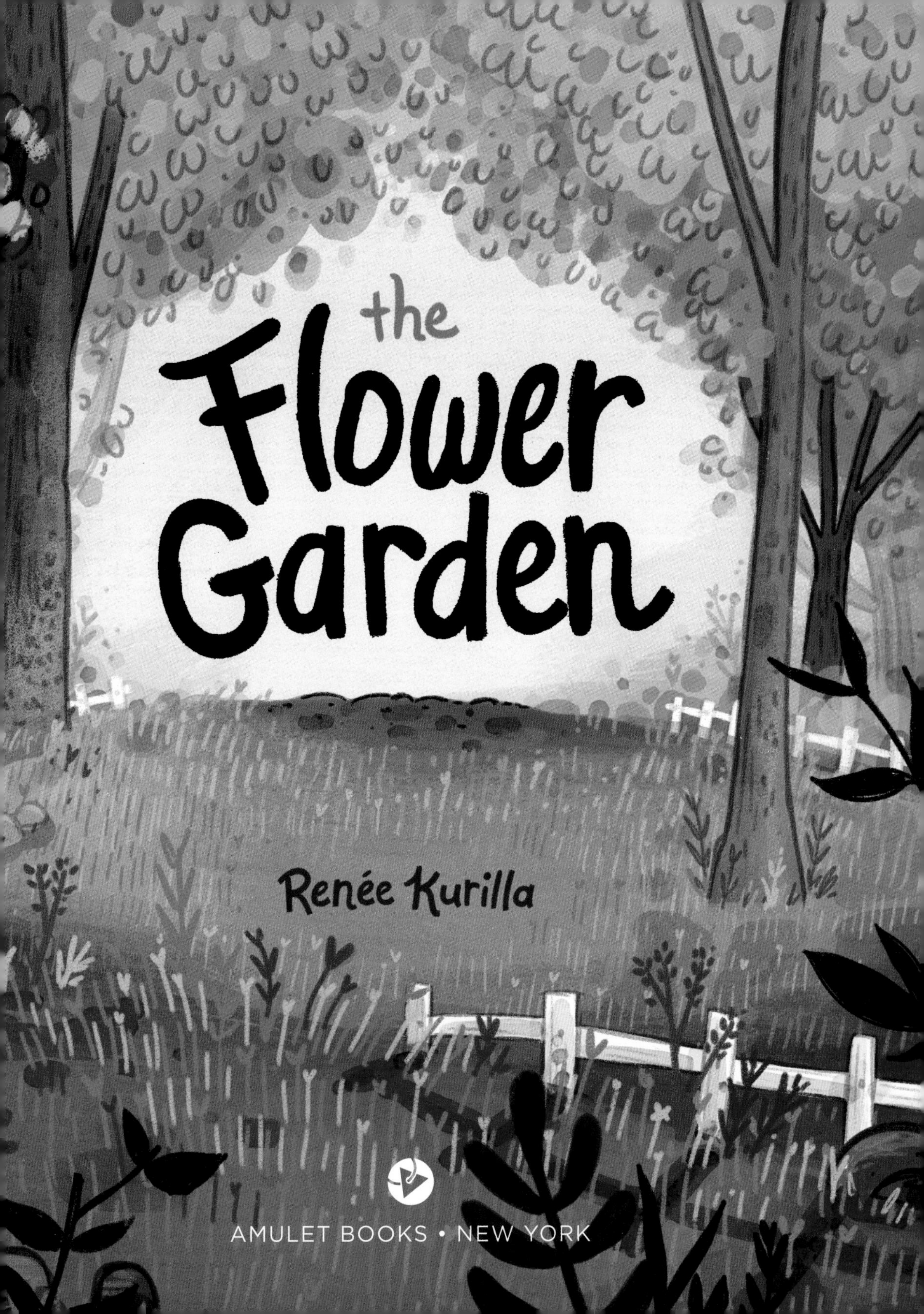

the Flower Garden

Renée Kurilla

AMULET BOOKS • NEW YORK

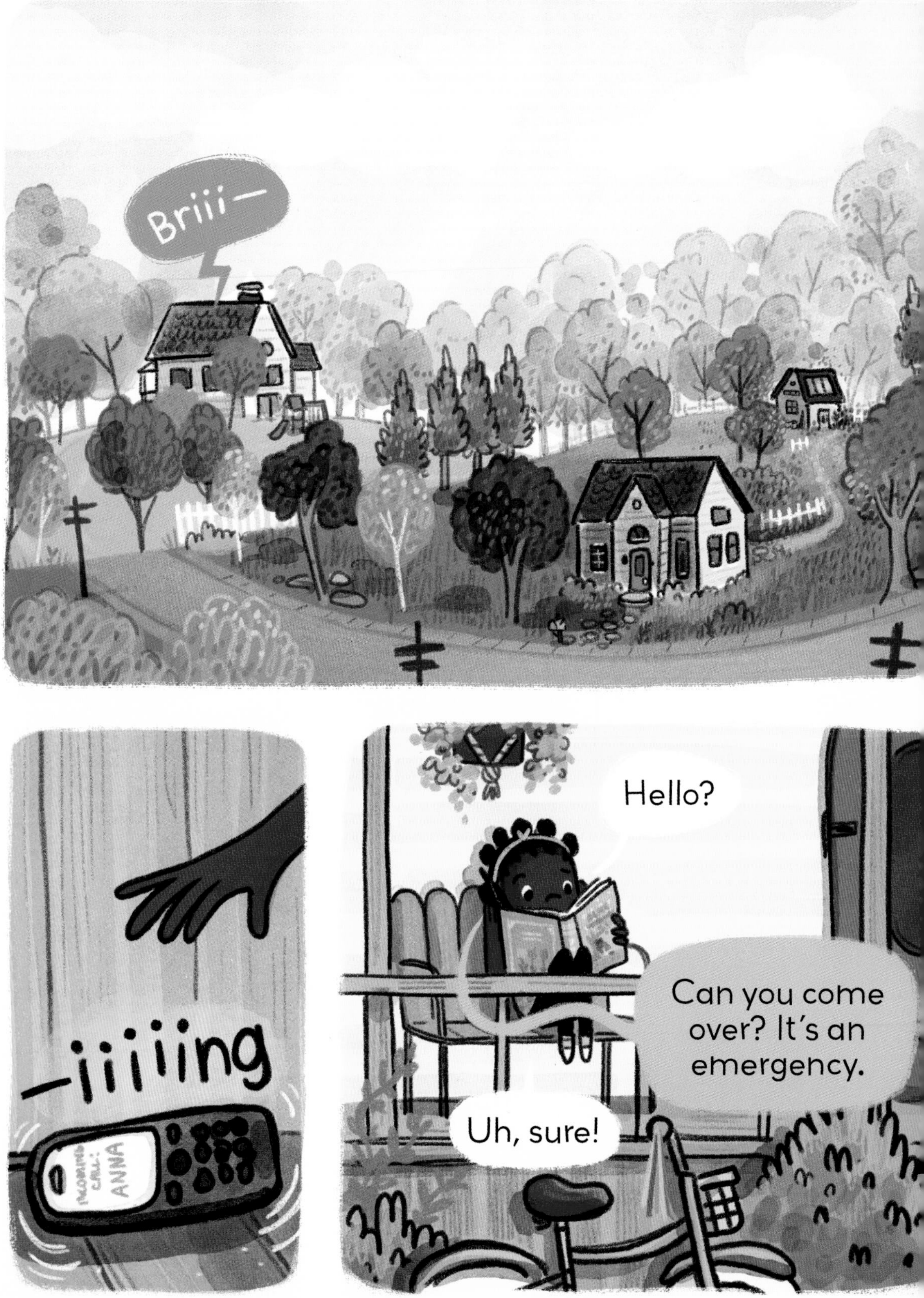
Briii—
—iiiing
INCOMING CALL: ANNA
Hello?
Can you come over? It's an emergency.
Uh, sure!

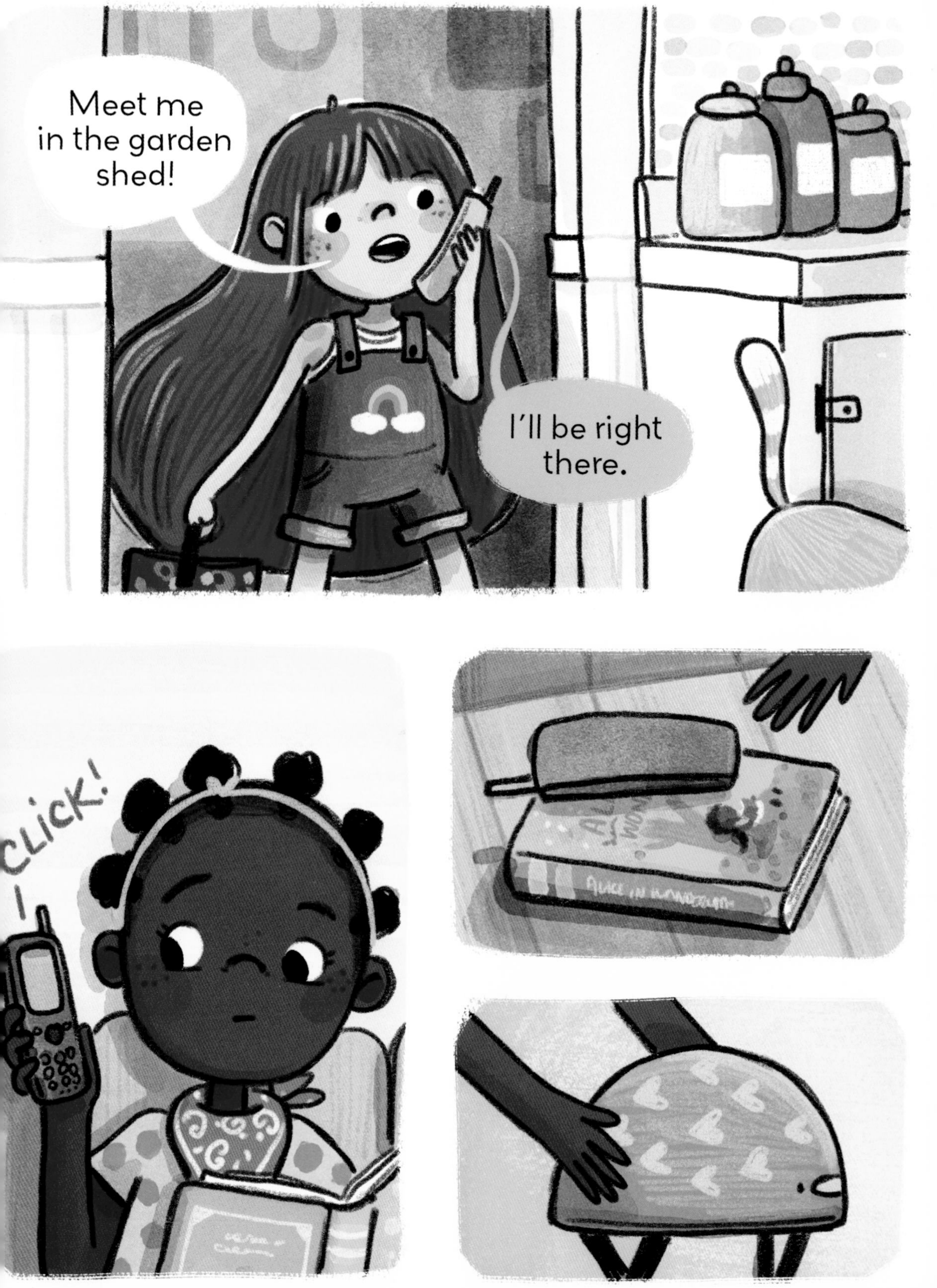
Meet me in the garden shed!
I'll be right there.
CLICK!
ALICE IN WONDERLAND

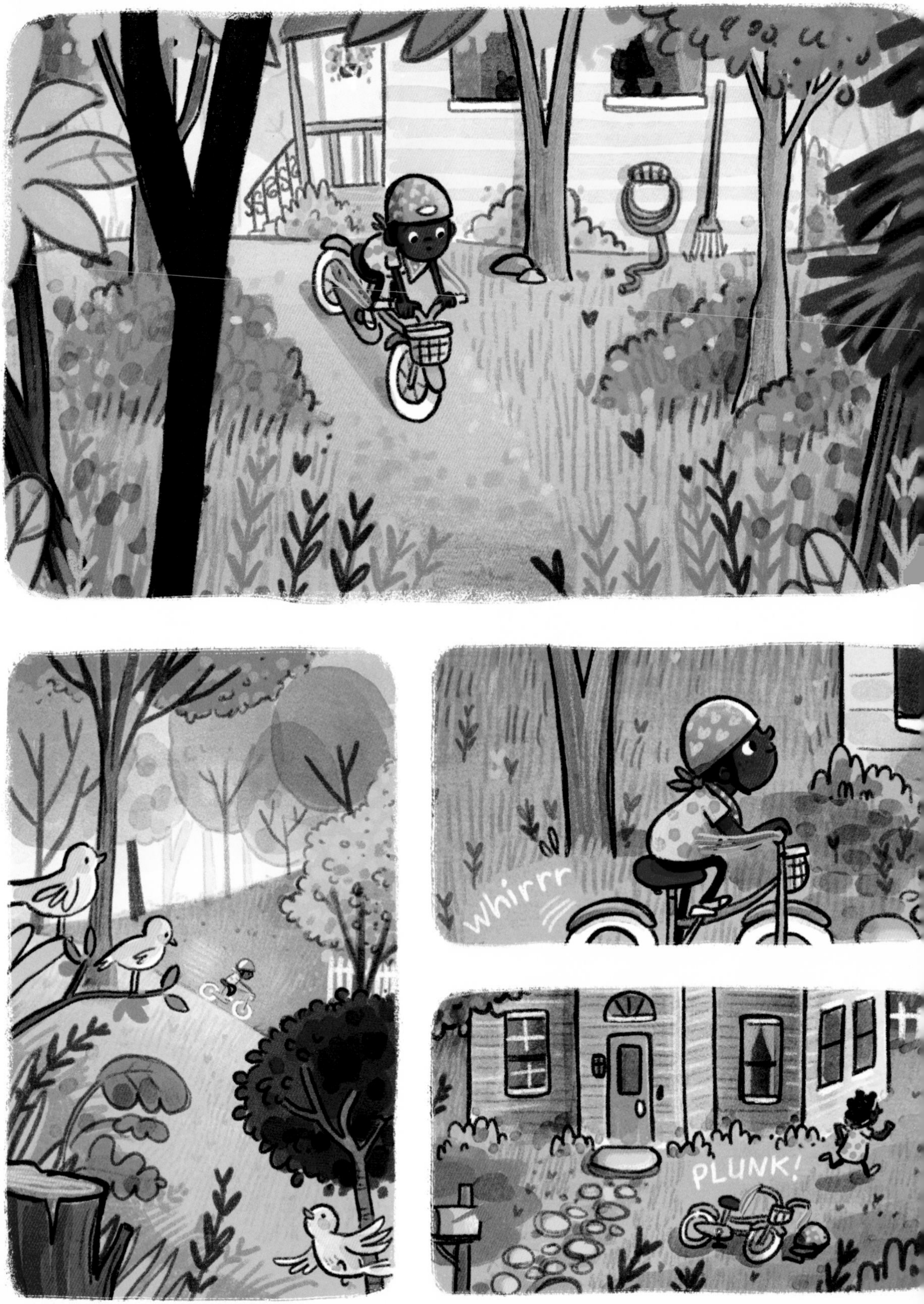
whirrr
PLUNK!

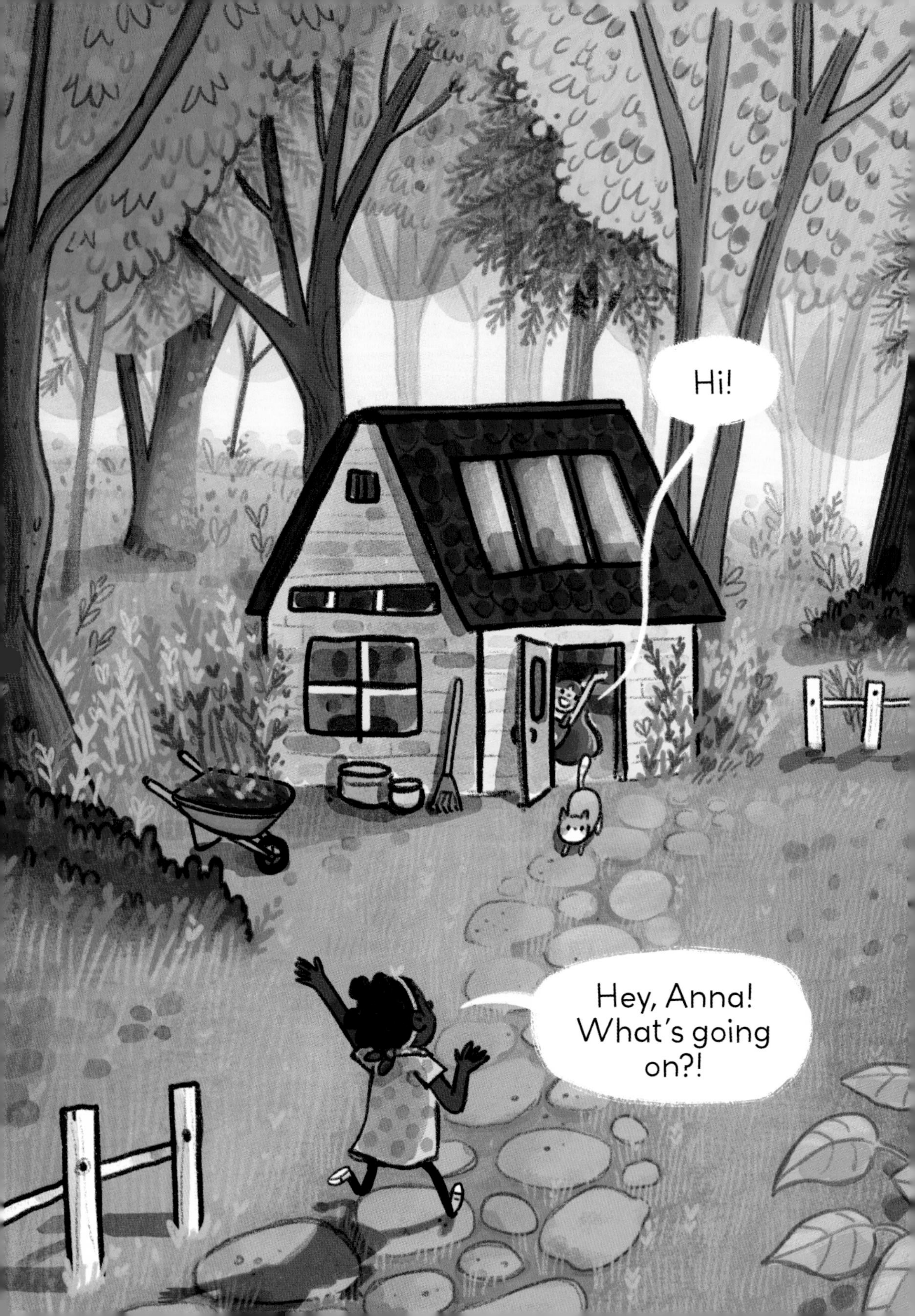
Hi!
Hey, Anna! What's going on?!

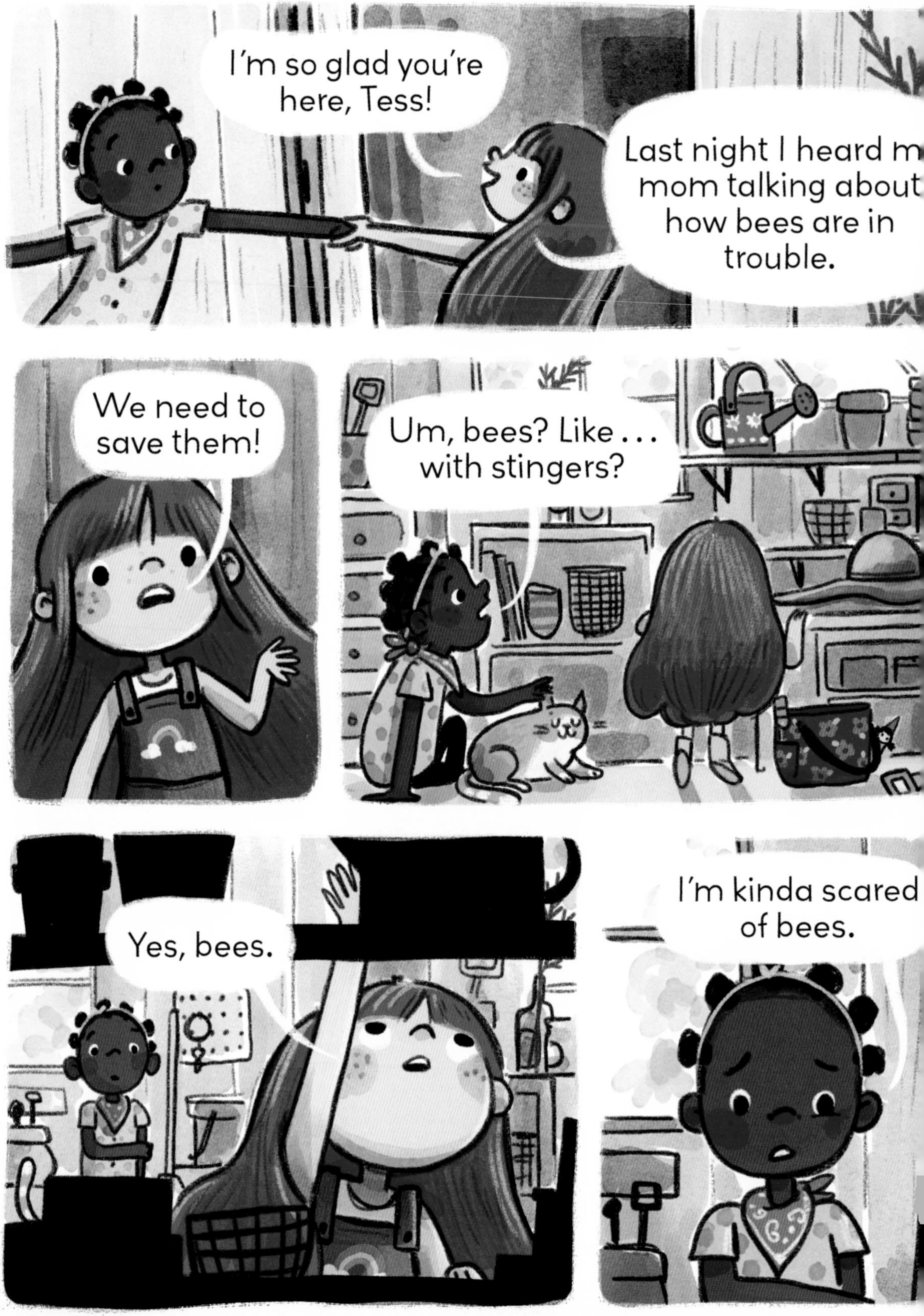
I'm so glad you're here, Tess!
Last night I heard m mom talking about how bees are in trouble.
We need to save them!
Um, bees? Like . . . with stingers?
Yes, bees.
I'm kinda scared of bees.

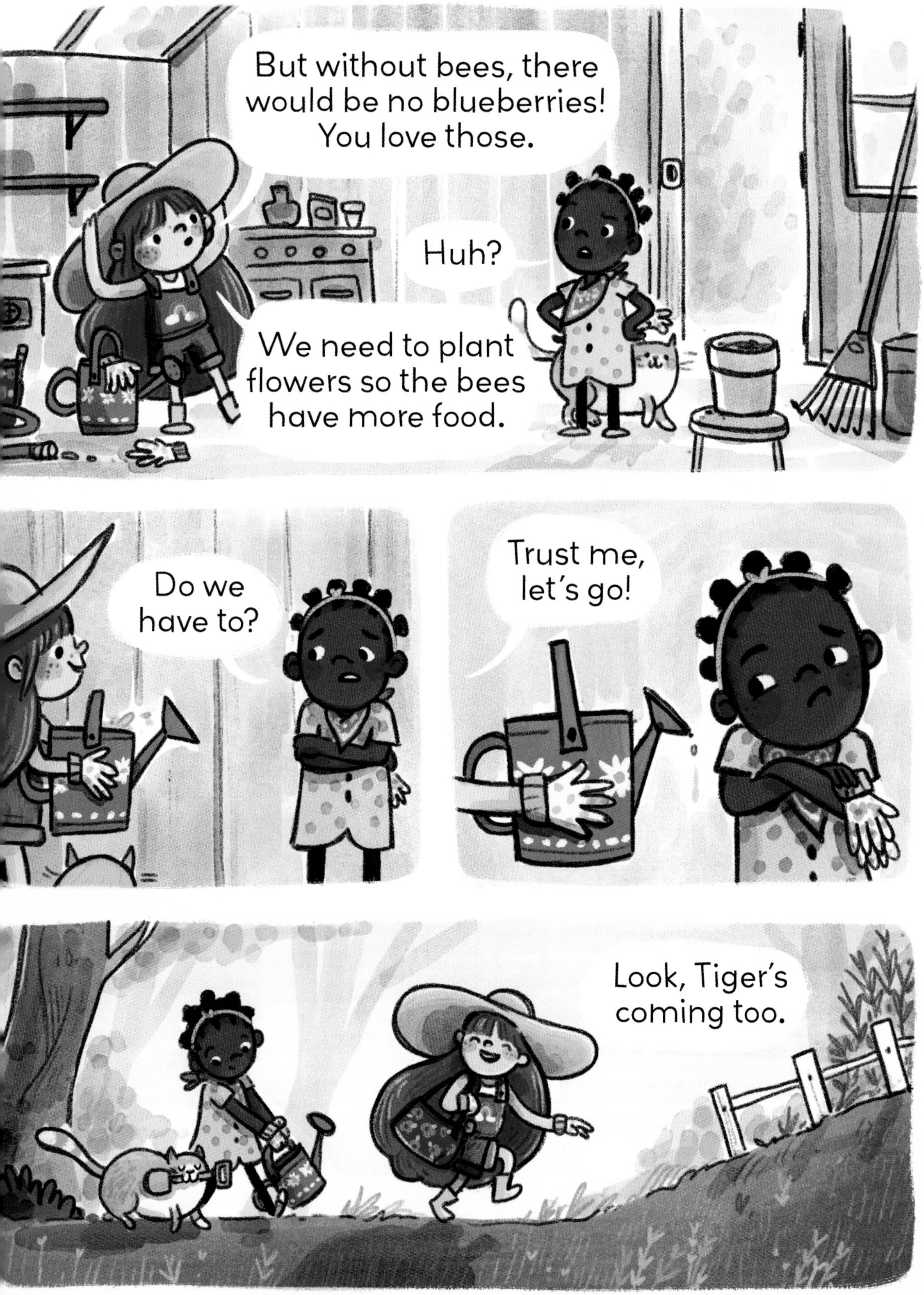
But without bees, there would be no blueberries! You love those.
Huh?
We need to plant flowers so the bees have more food.
Do we have to?
Trust me, let's go!
Look, Tiger's coming too.

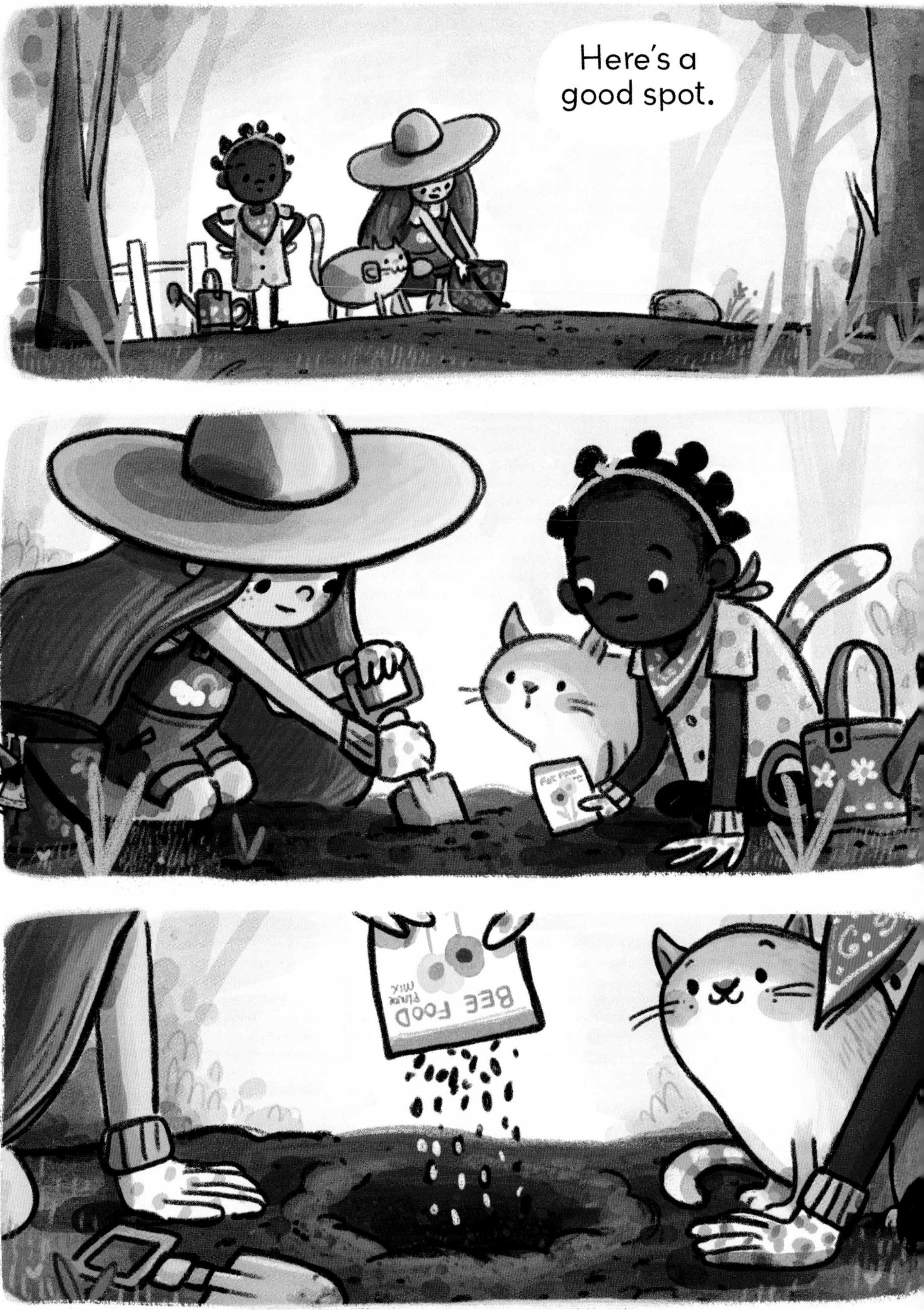
Here's a good spot.
BEE FOOD

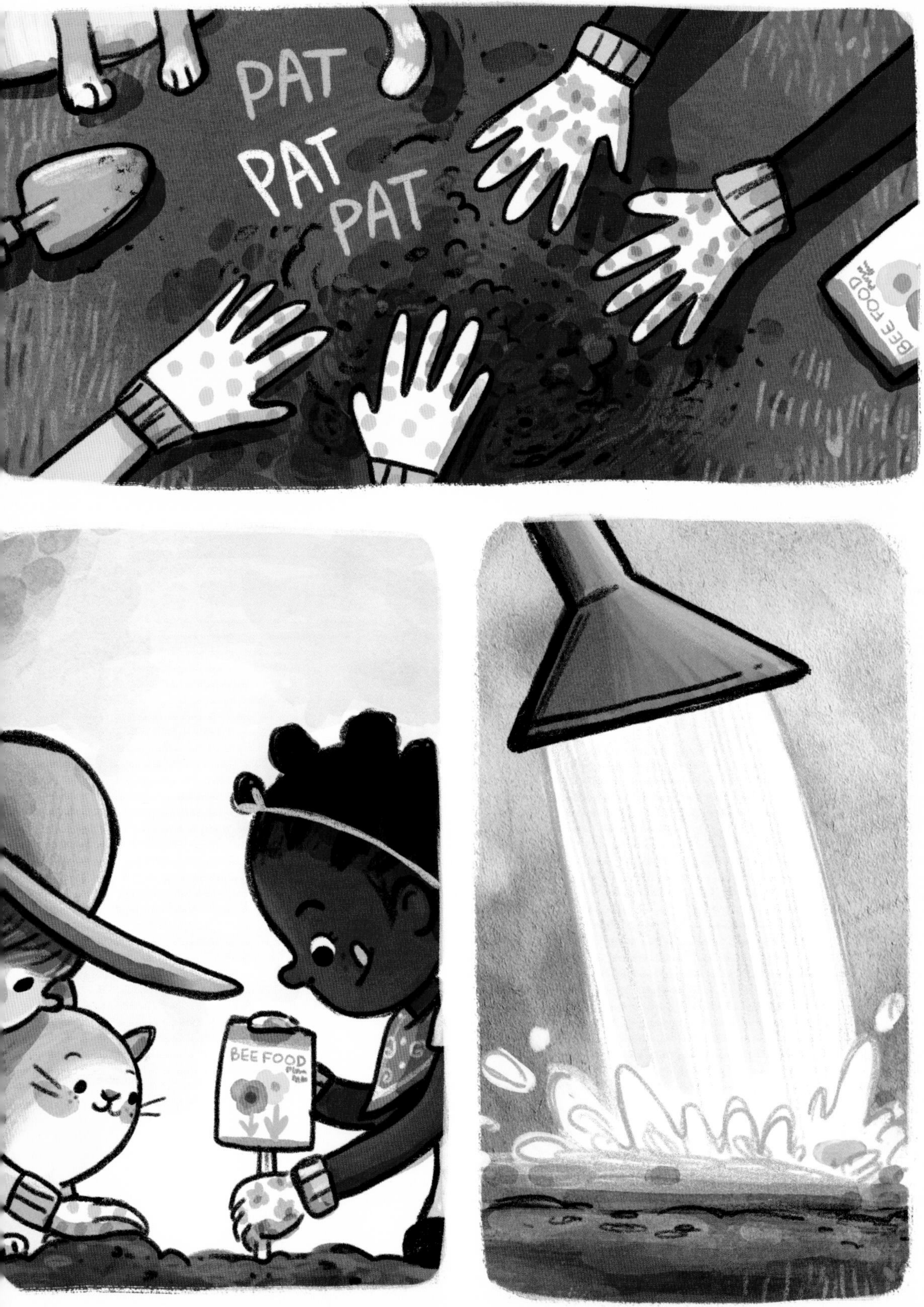
PAT
PAT
PAT
BEE FOOD
BEE FOOD

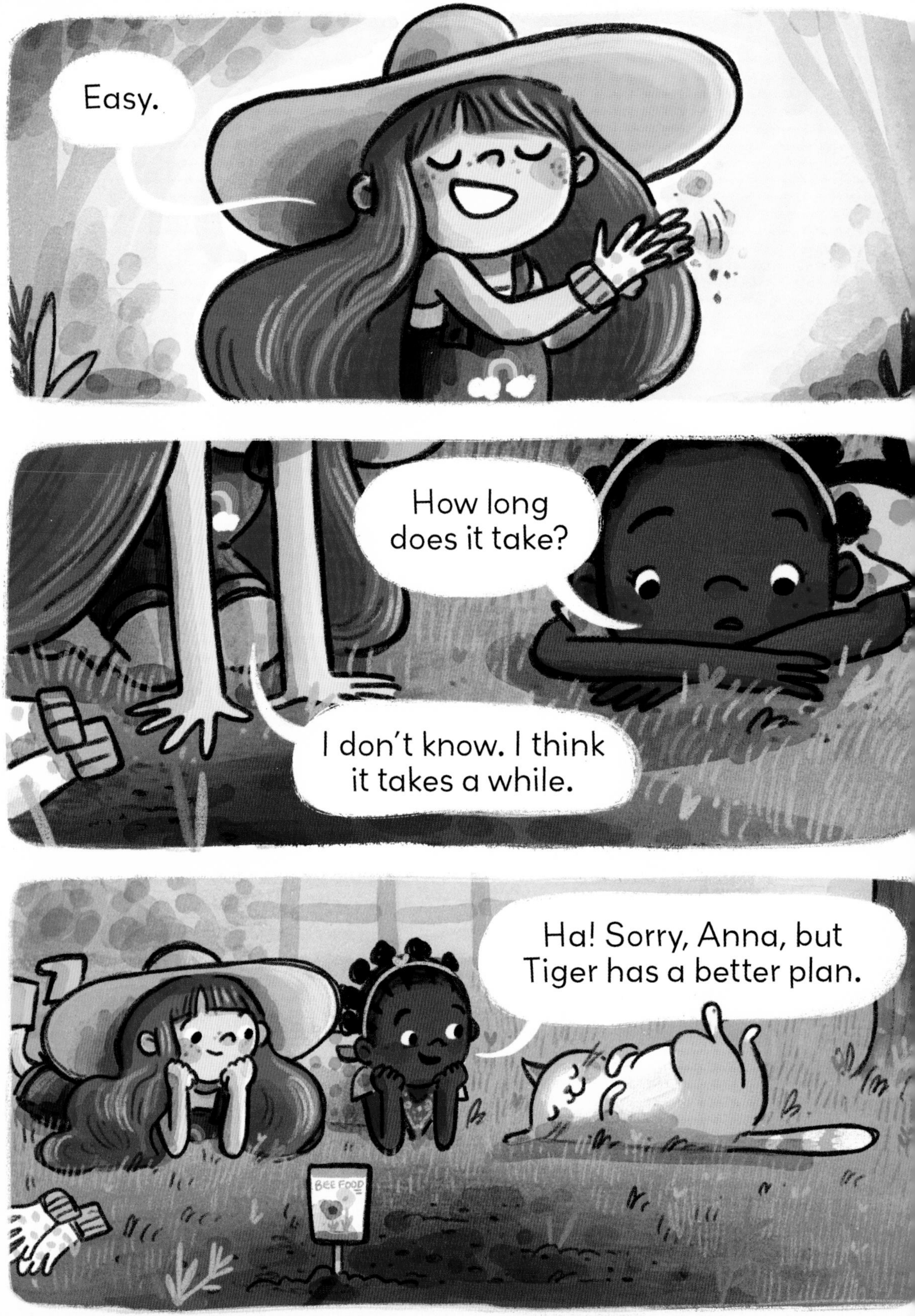
Easy.
How long does it take?
I don't know. I think it takes a while.
Ha! Sorry, Anna, but Tiger has a better plan.
BEE FOOD

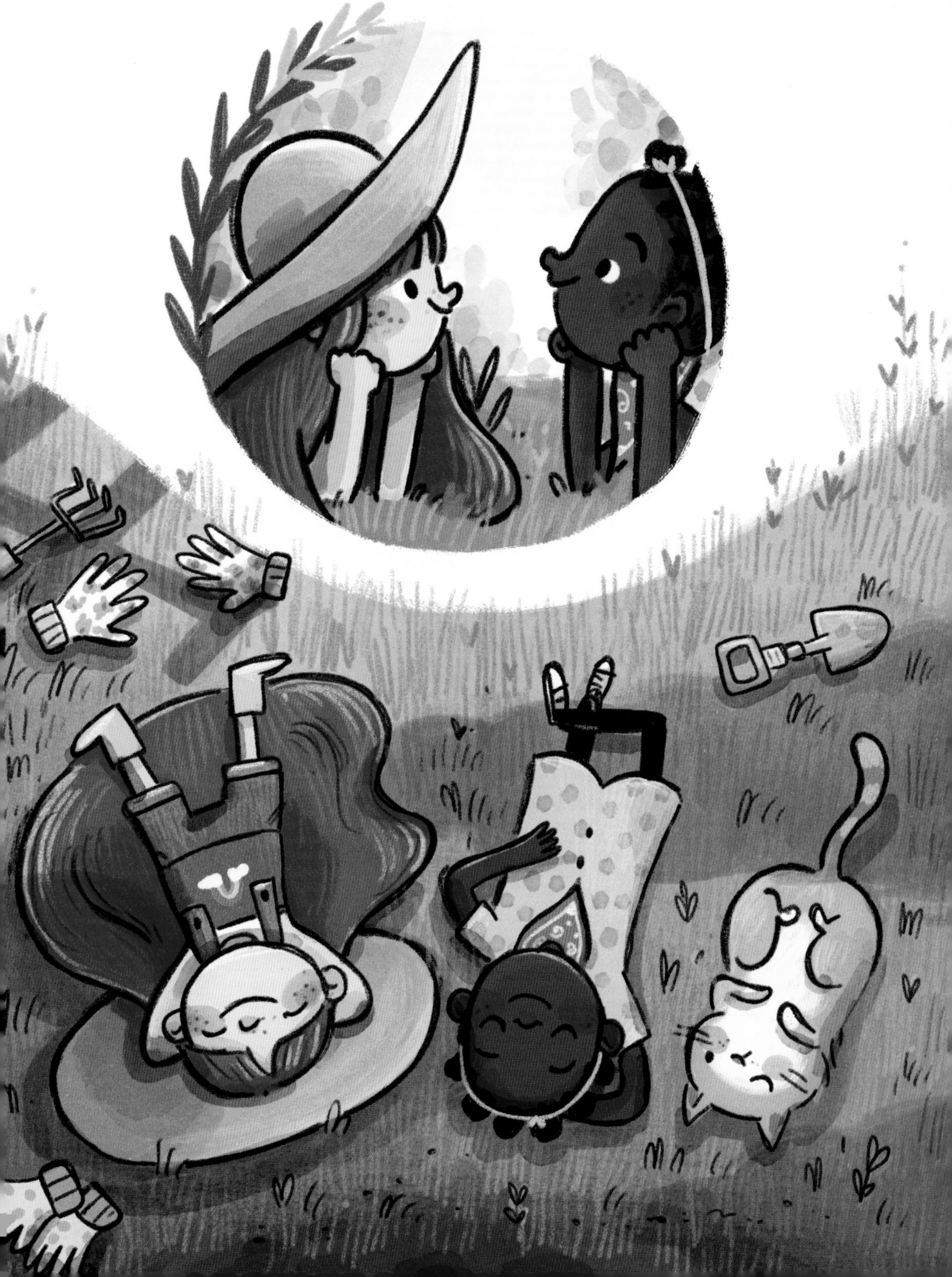

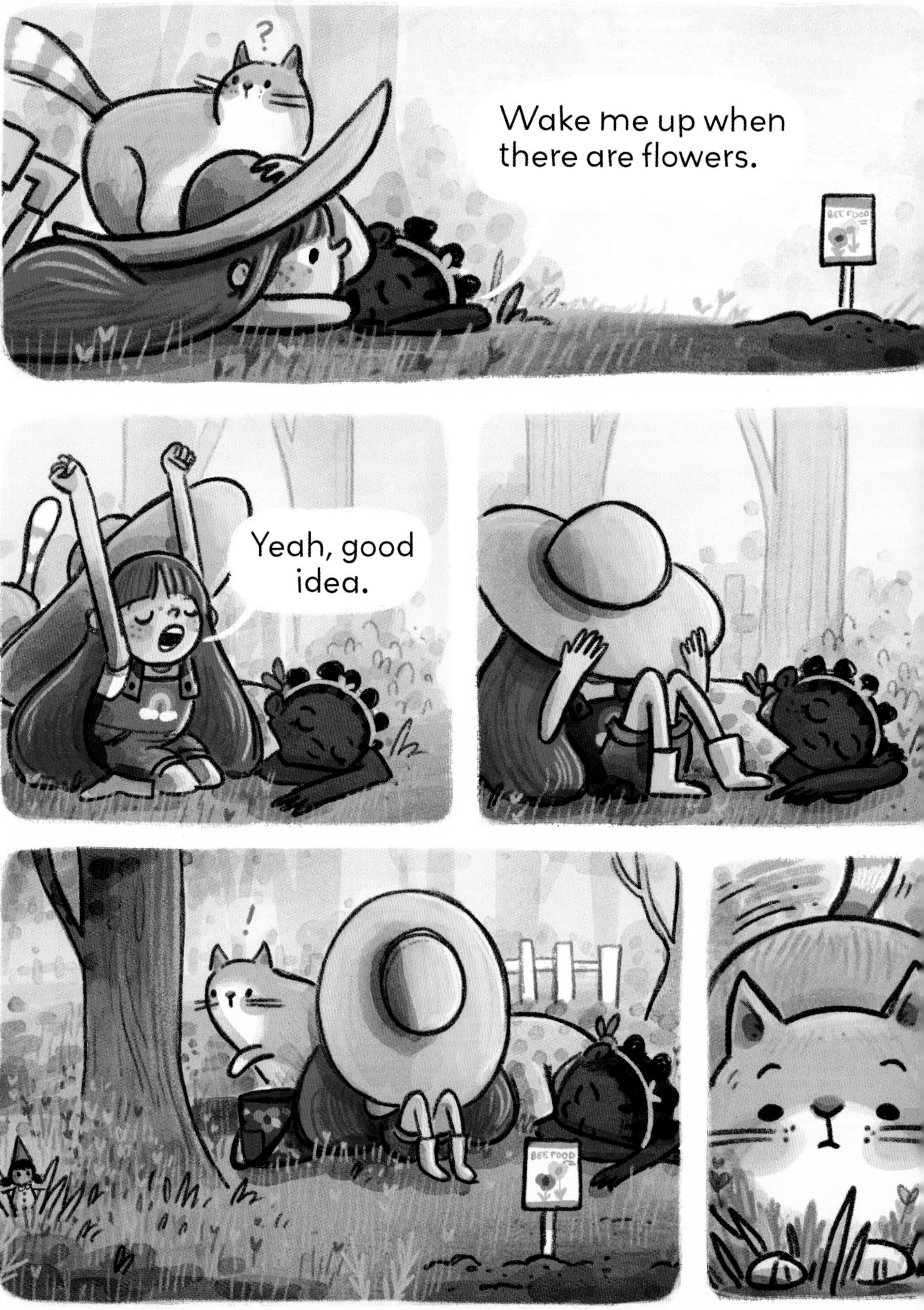
?
Wake me up when there are flowers.
BEE FOOD
Yeah, good idea.
!
BEE FOOD

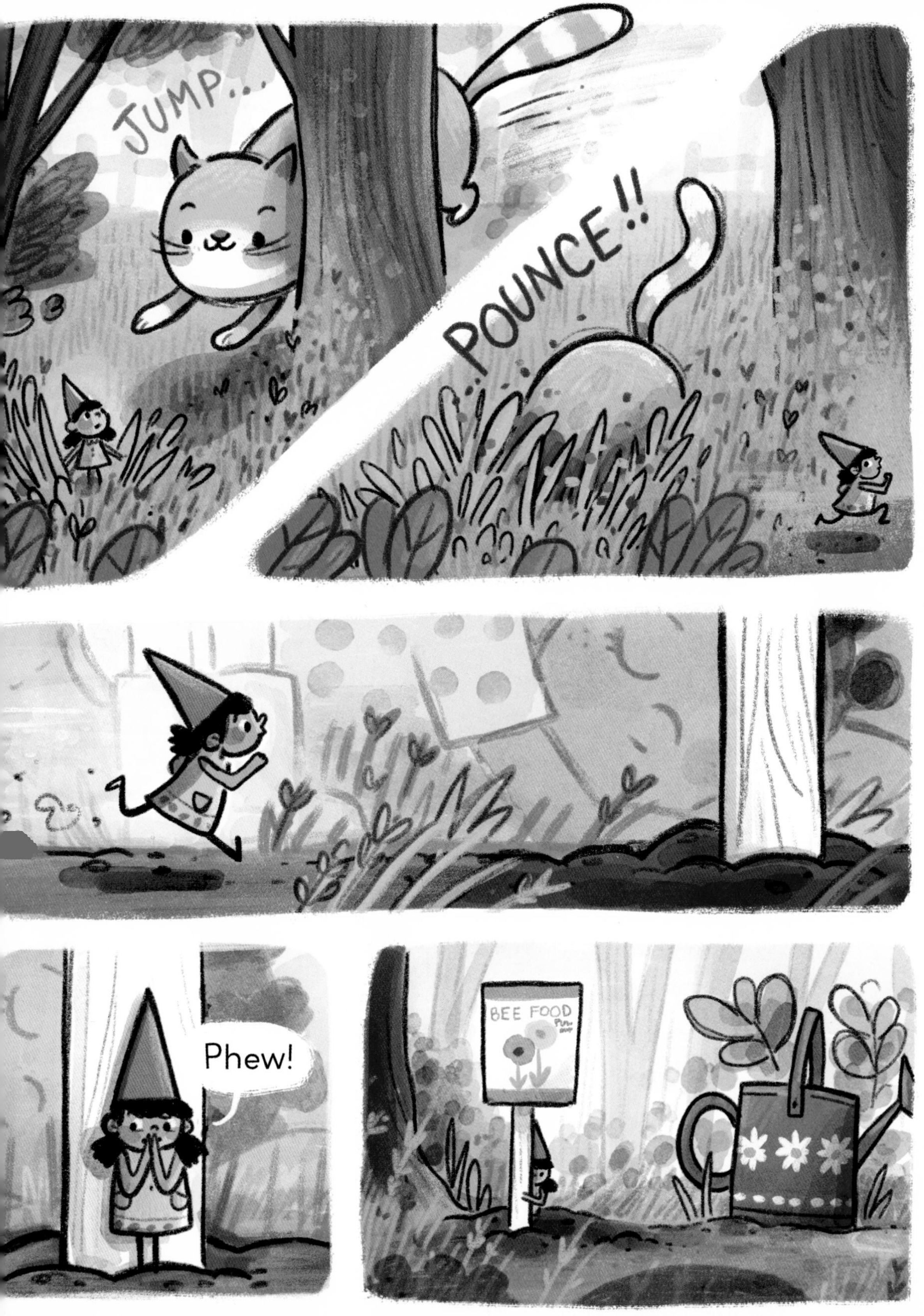
JUMP...
POUNCE!!
Phew!
BEE FOOD

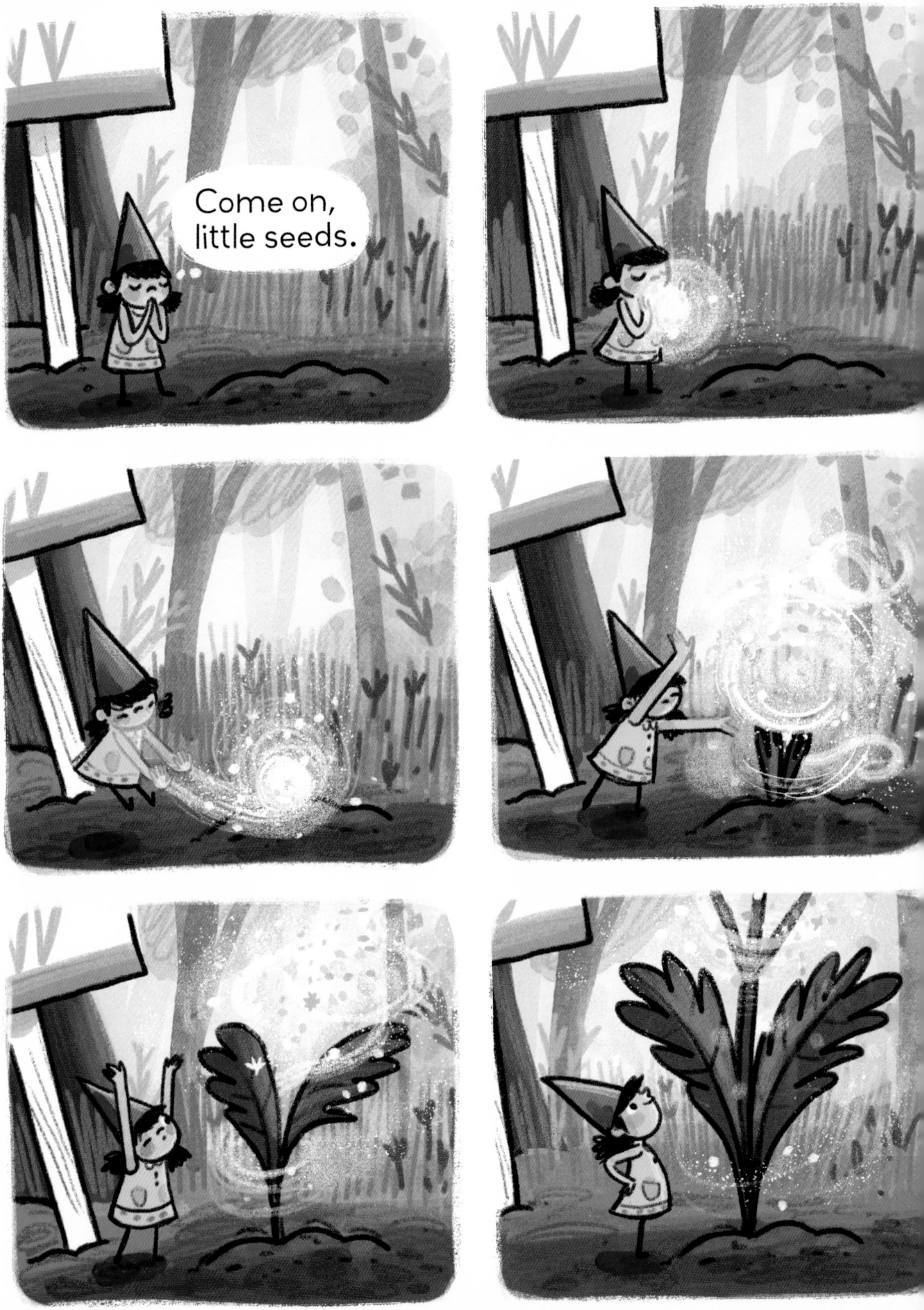
Come on, little seeds.

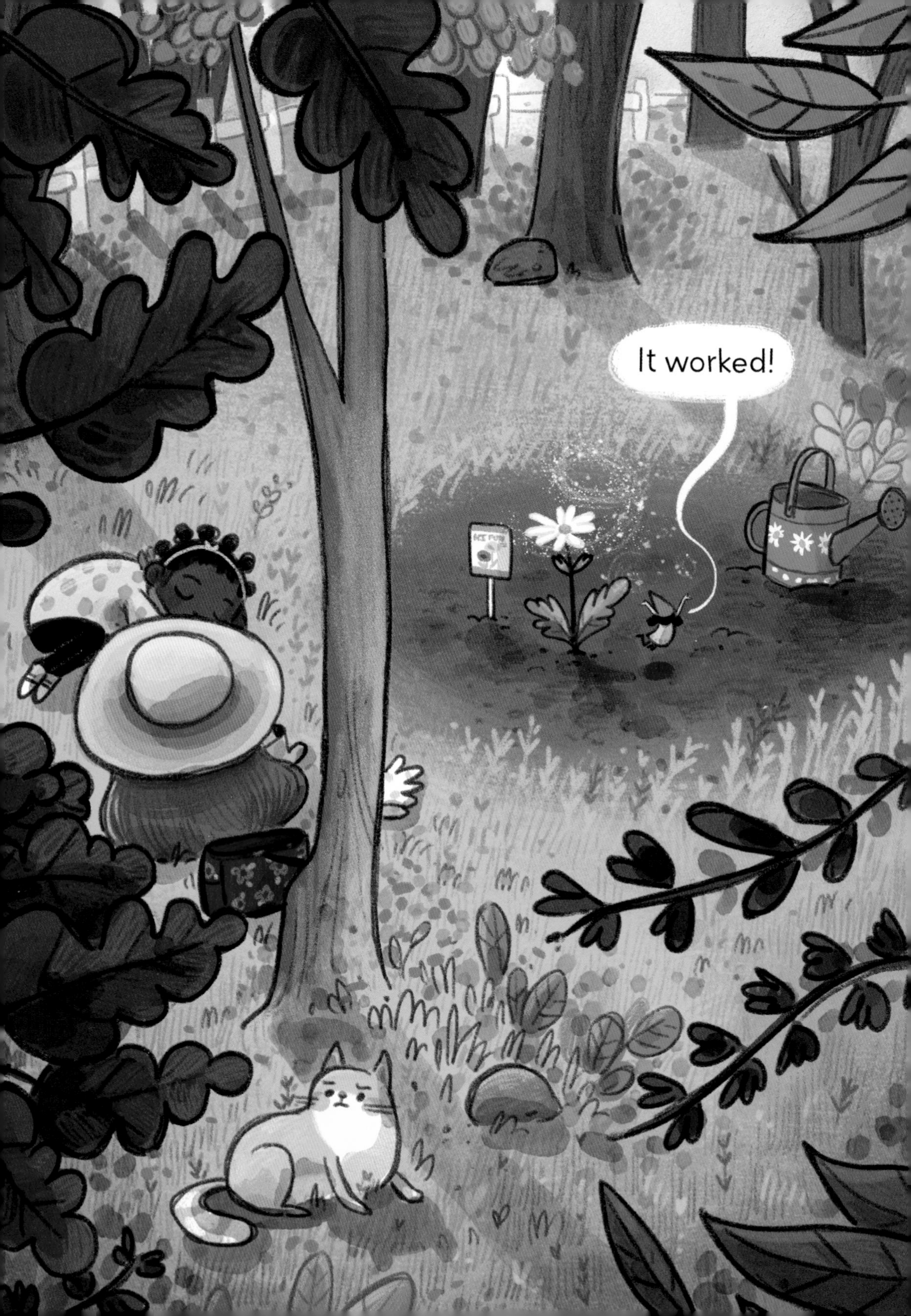
It worked!

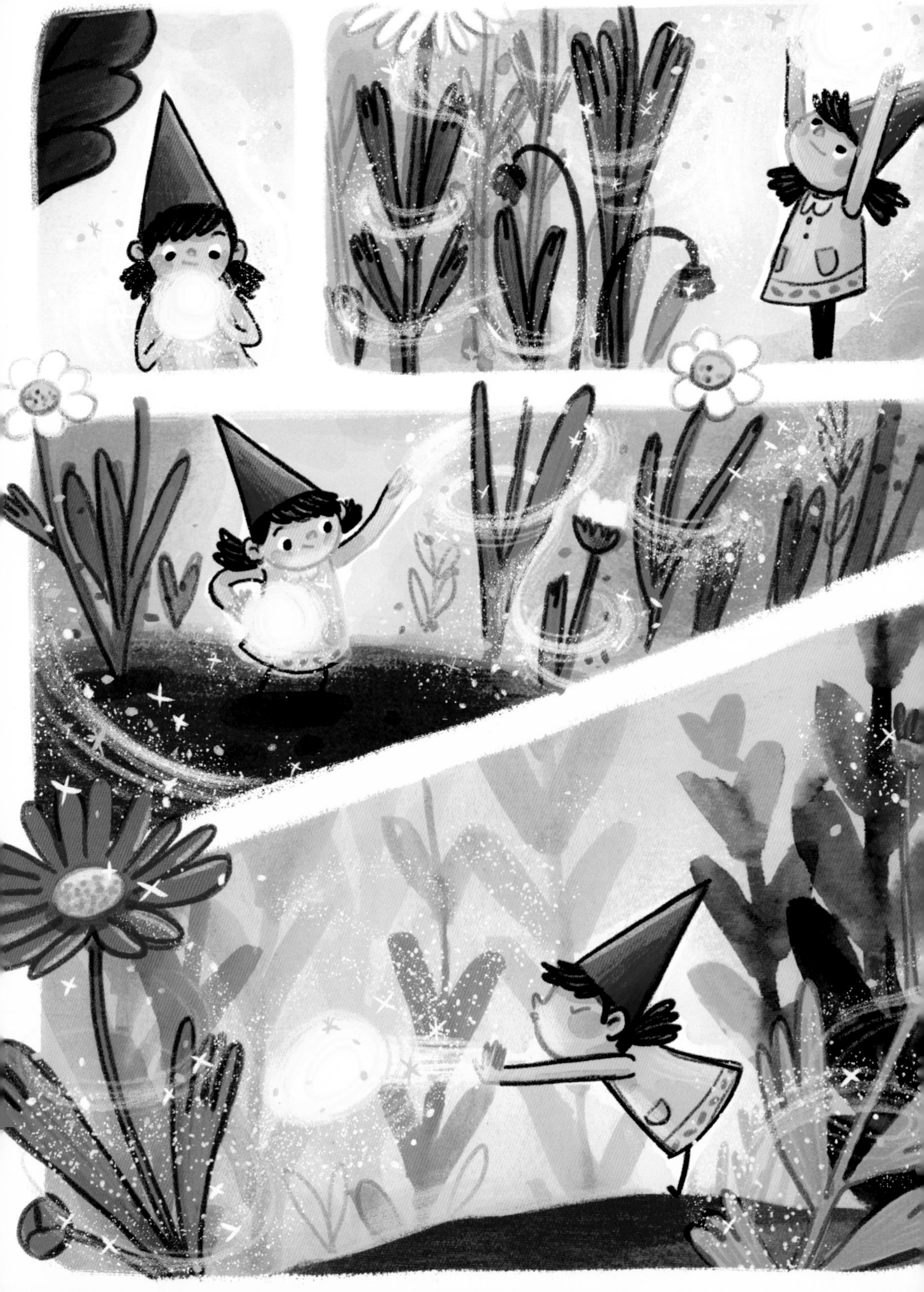

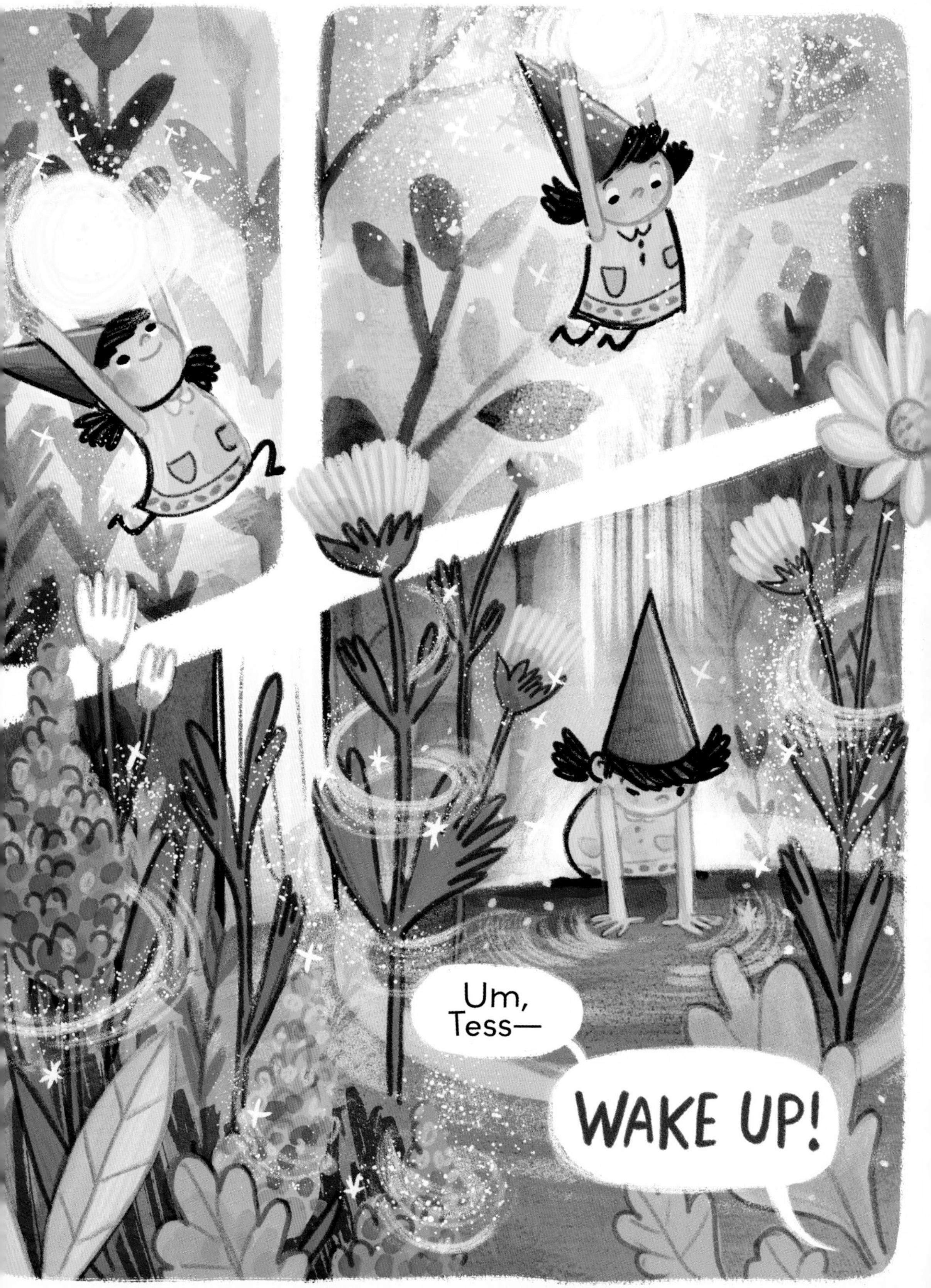
Um, Tess—
WAKE UP!

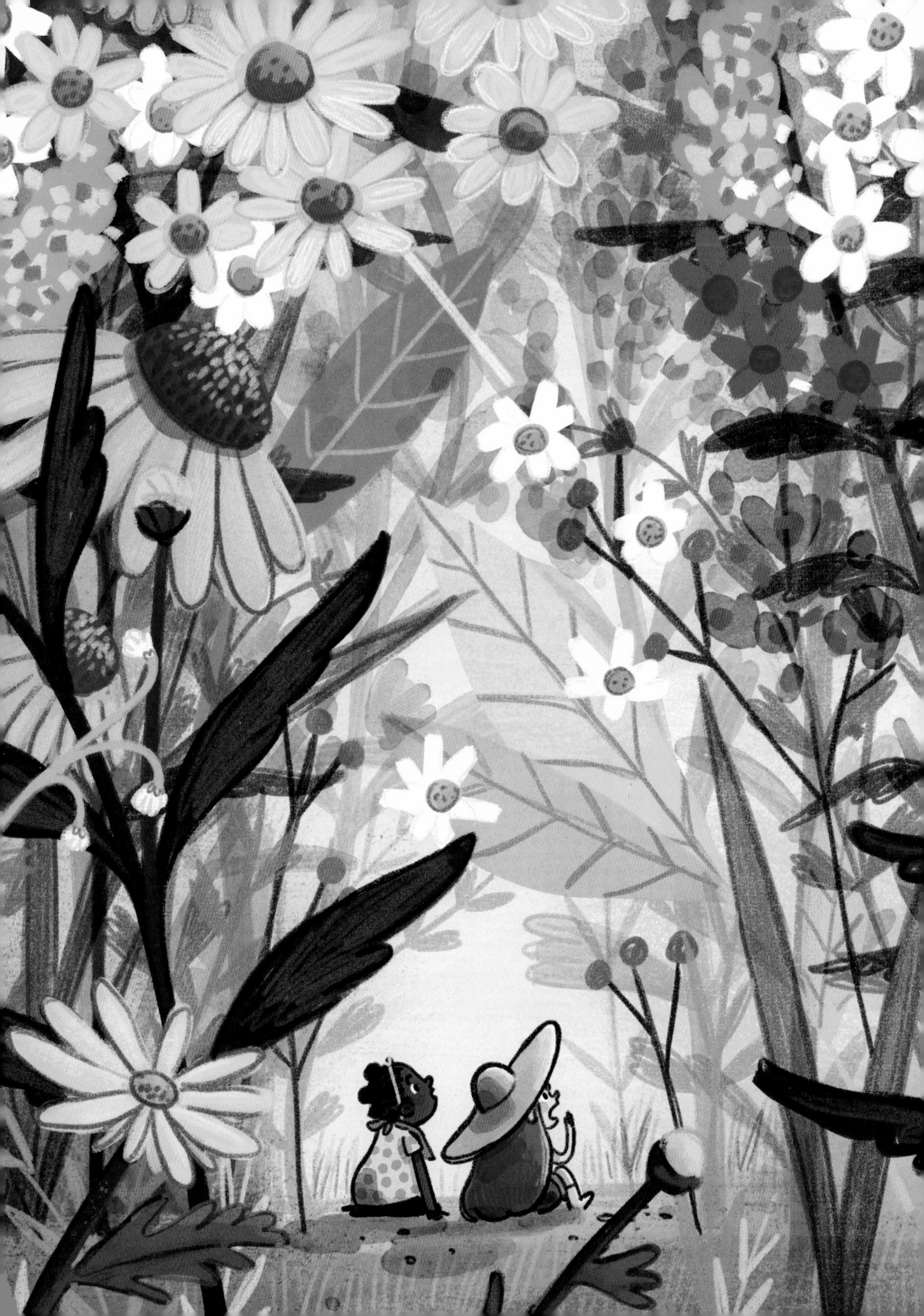

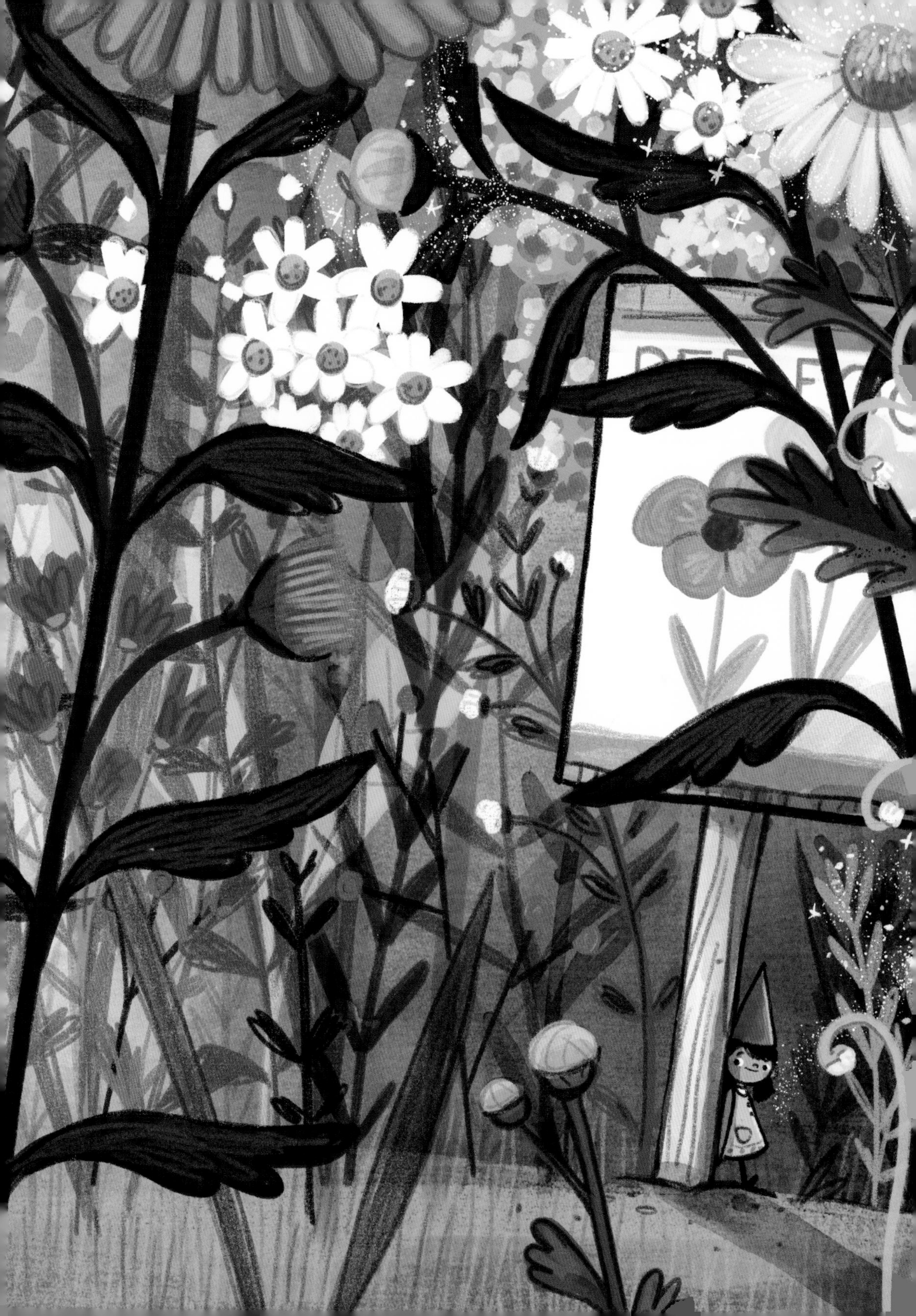

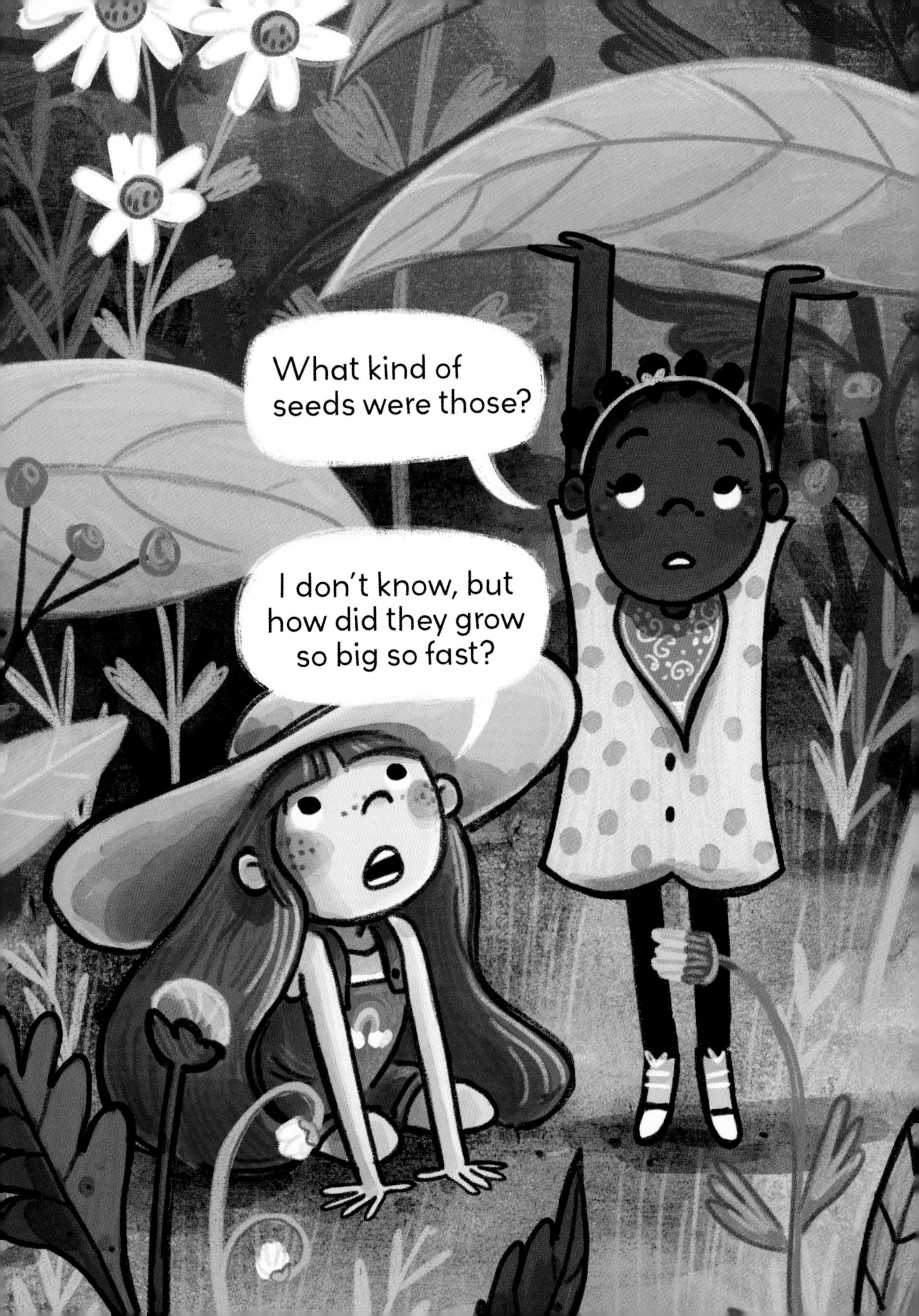
What kind of seeds were those?
I don't know, but how did they grow so big so fast?

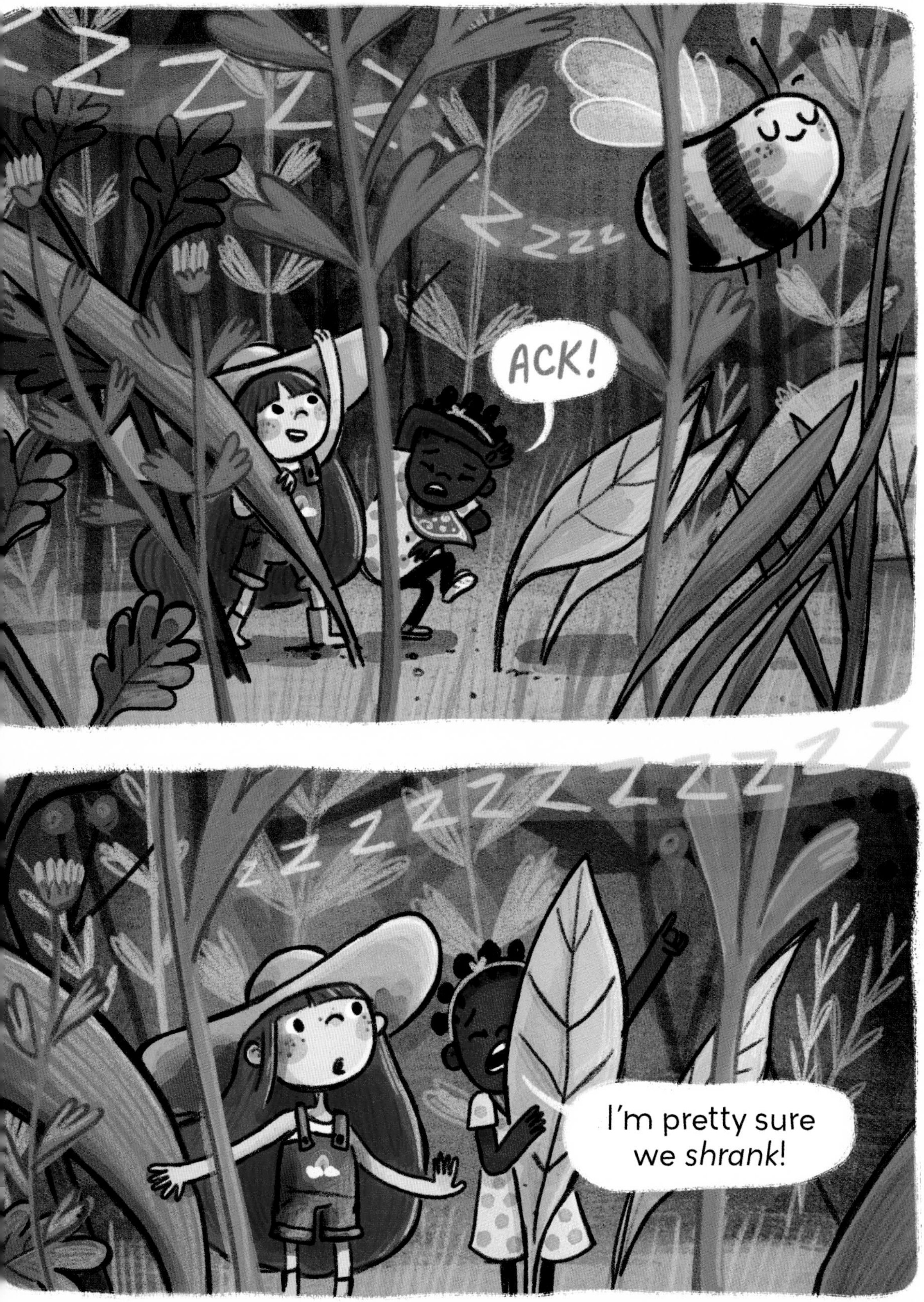
Zzzz
ACK!
ZZZZZZZZZZZ
I'm pretty sure we *shrank*!

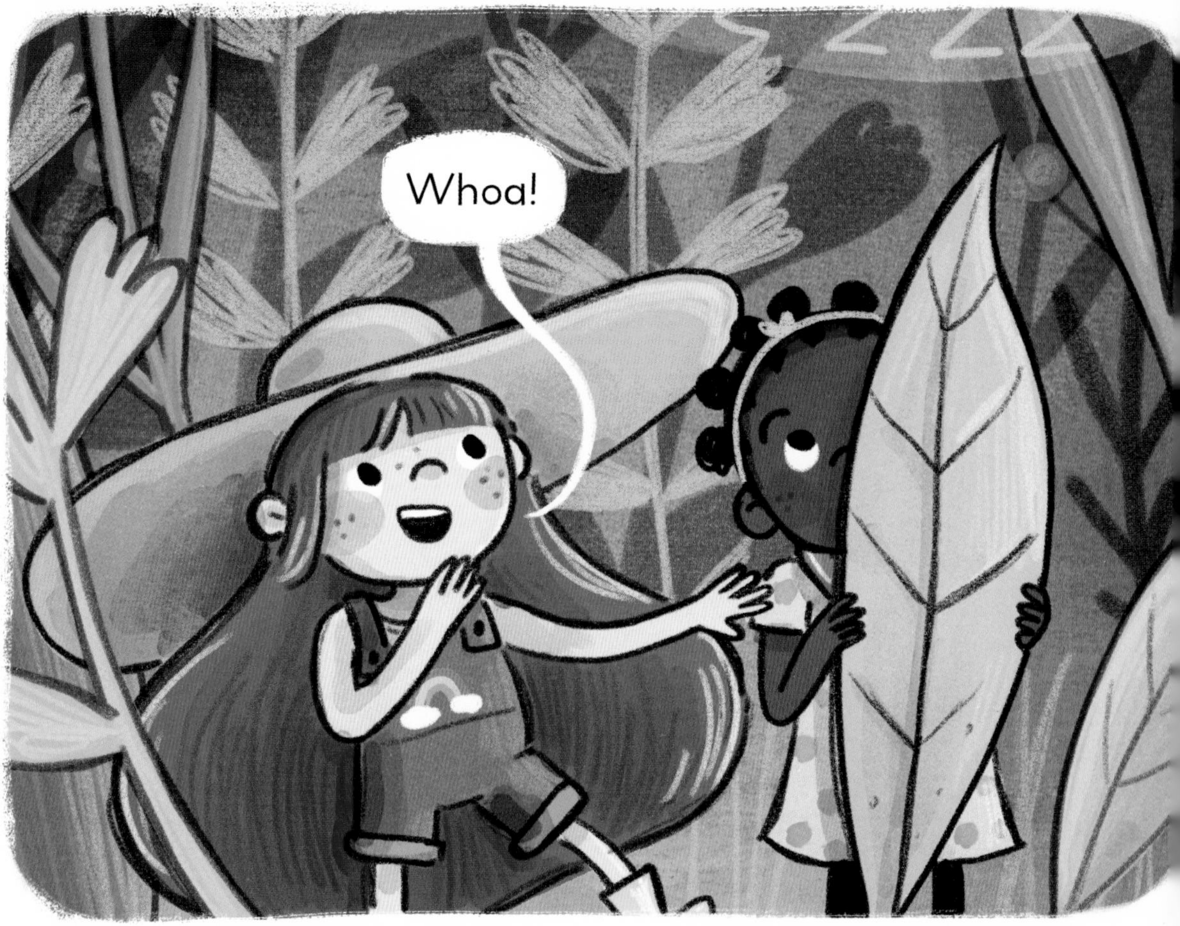
Whoa!

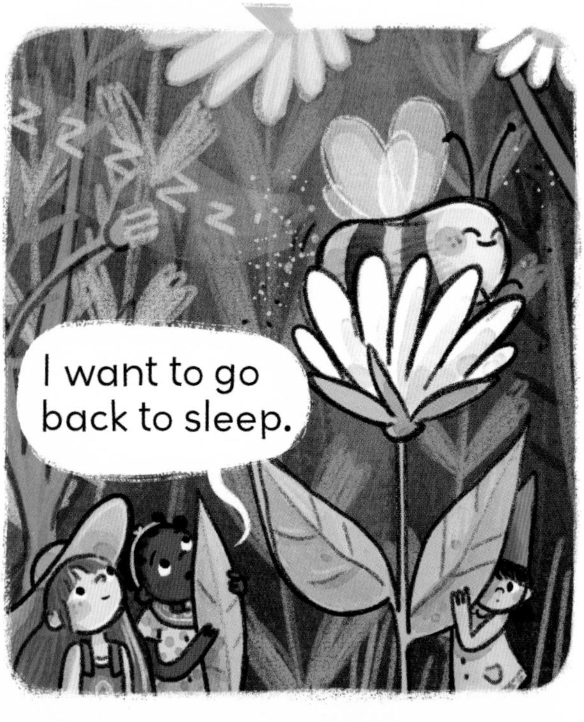
I want to go back to sleep.

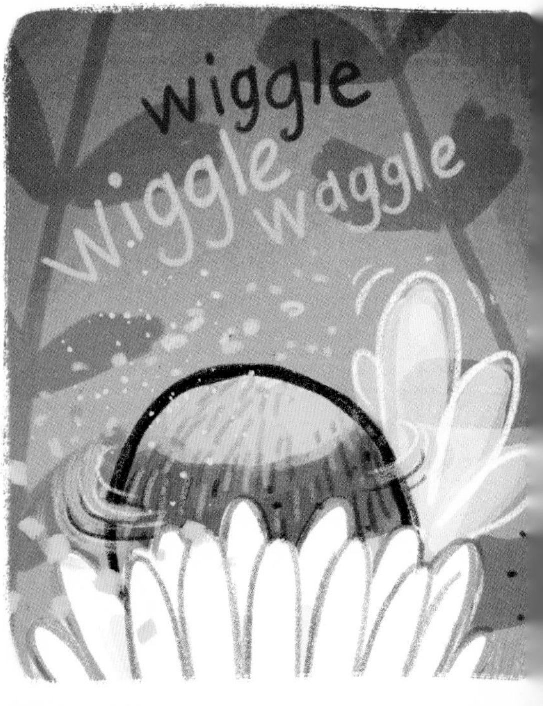
wiggle
wiggle
waggle

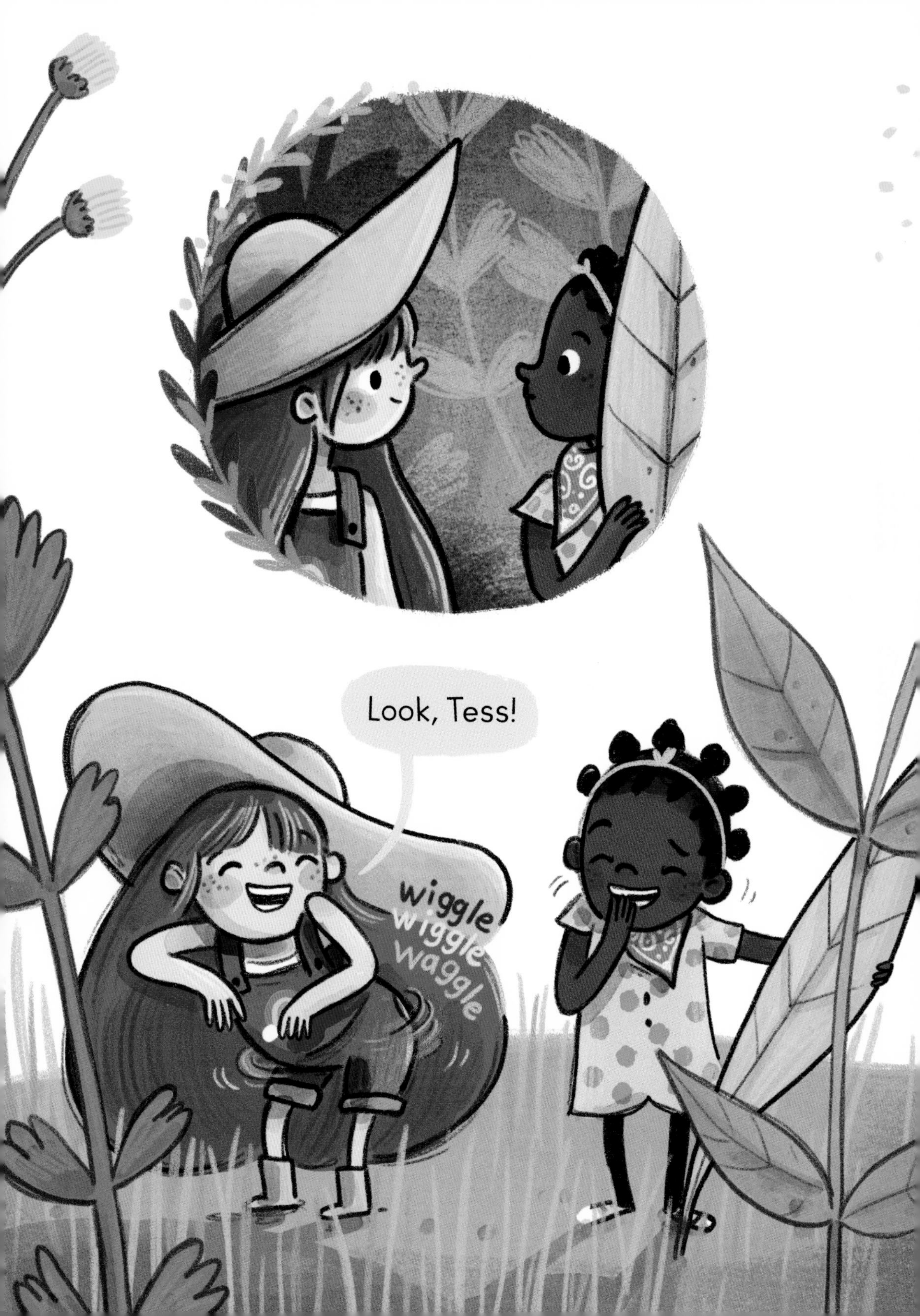
Look, Tess!
wiggle
wiggle
waggle

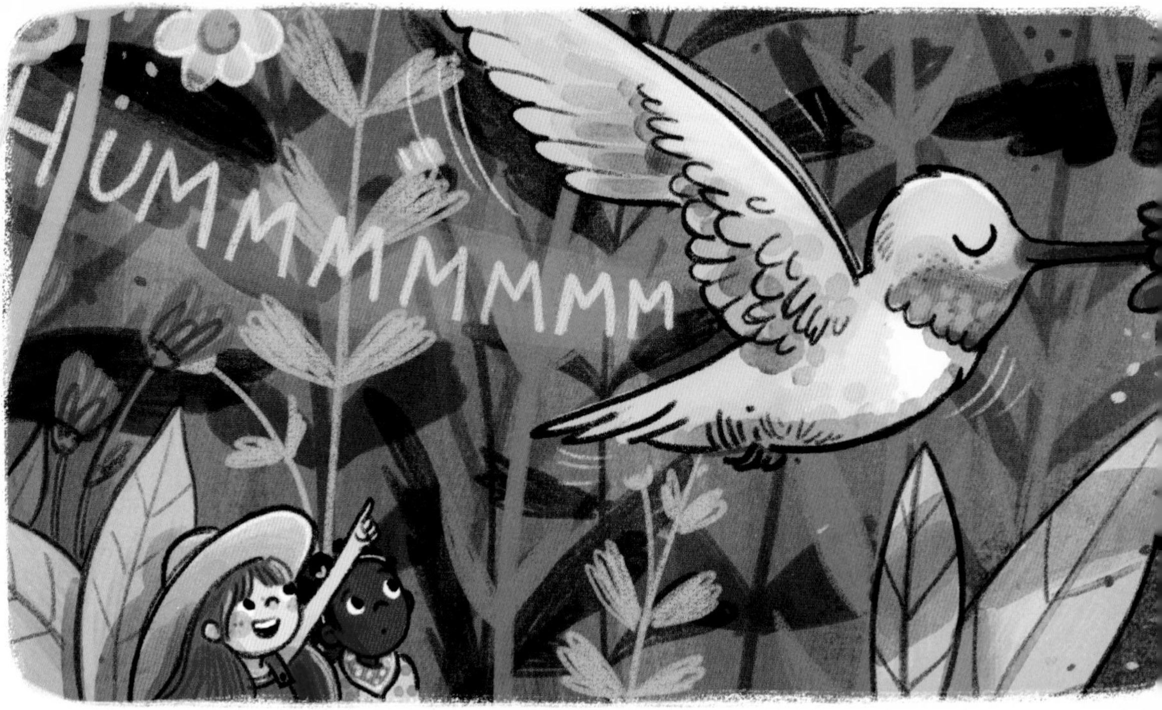
HUMMMMMMMM

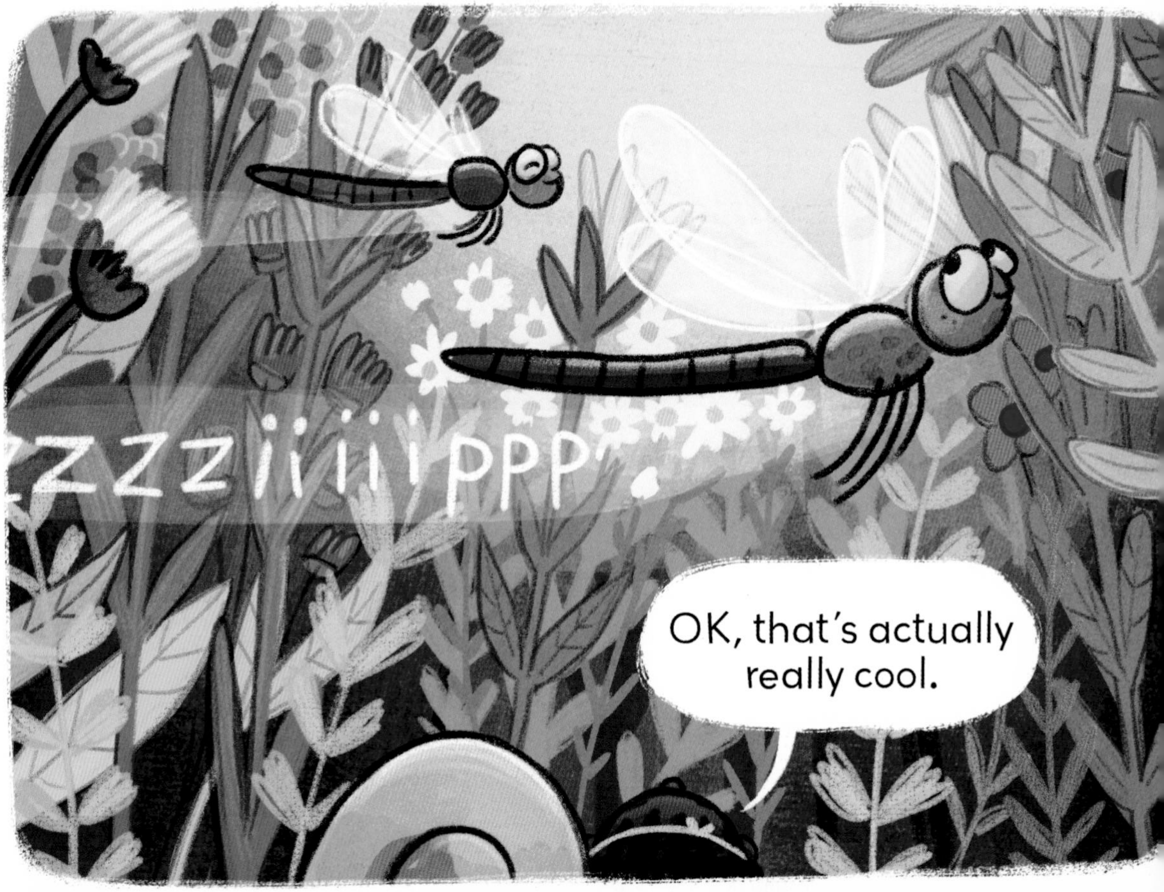
ZZZZiiiiPPP
OK, that's actually really cool.

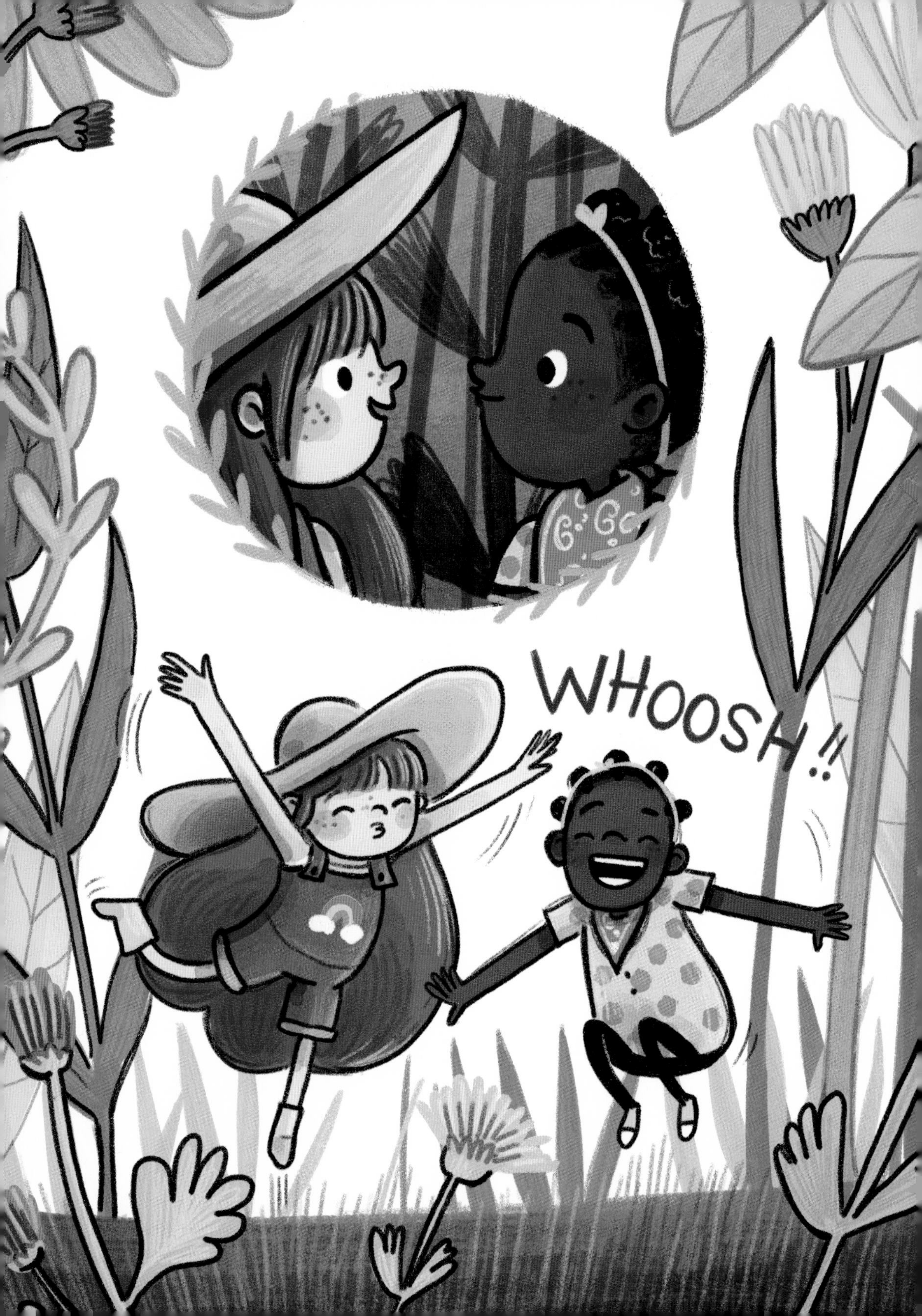
WHOOSH!!

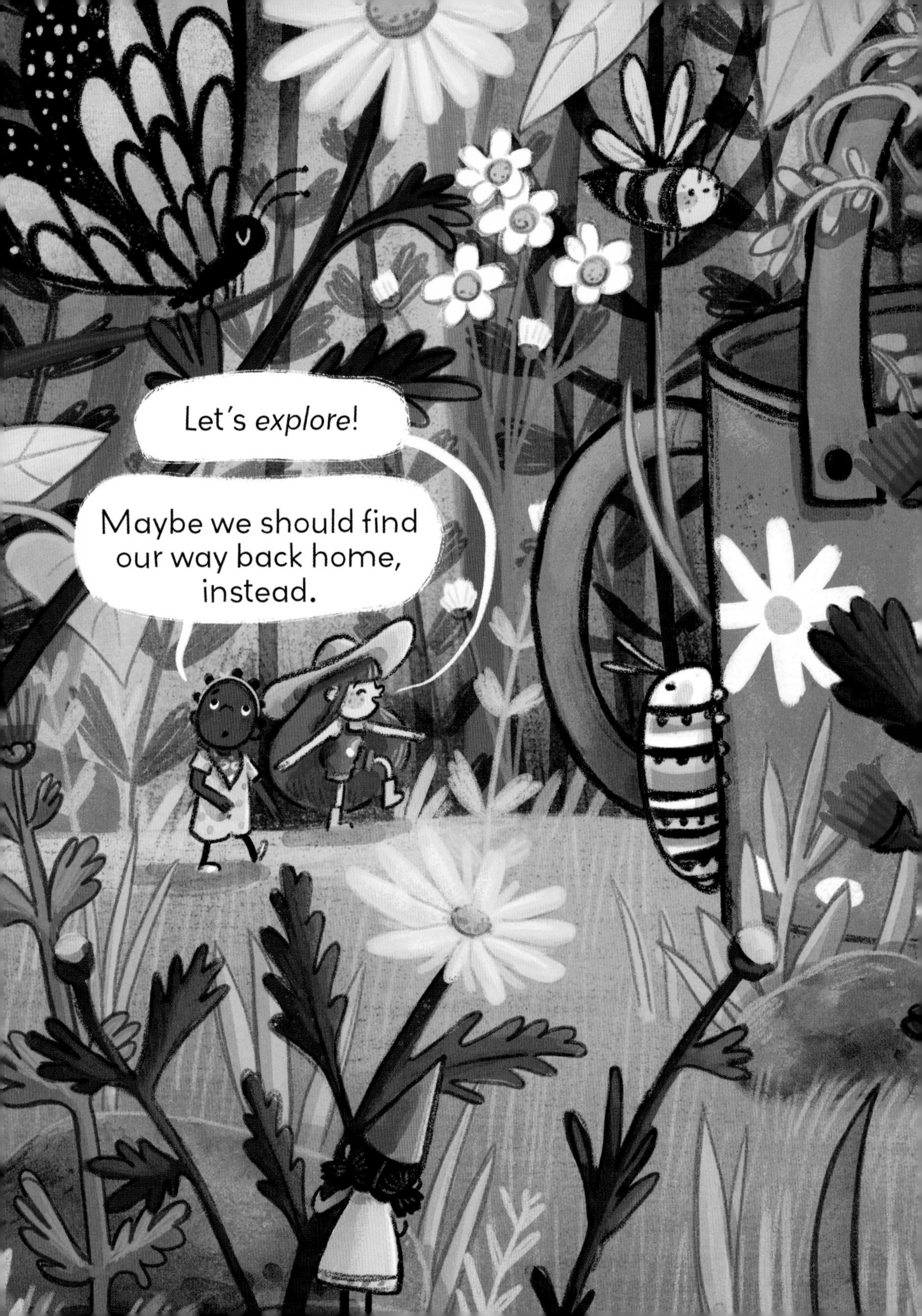
Let's *explore*!
Maybe we should find our way back home, instead.

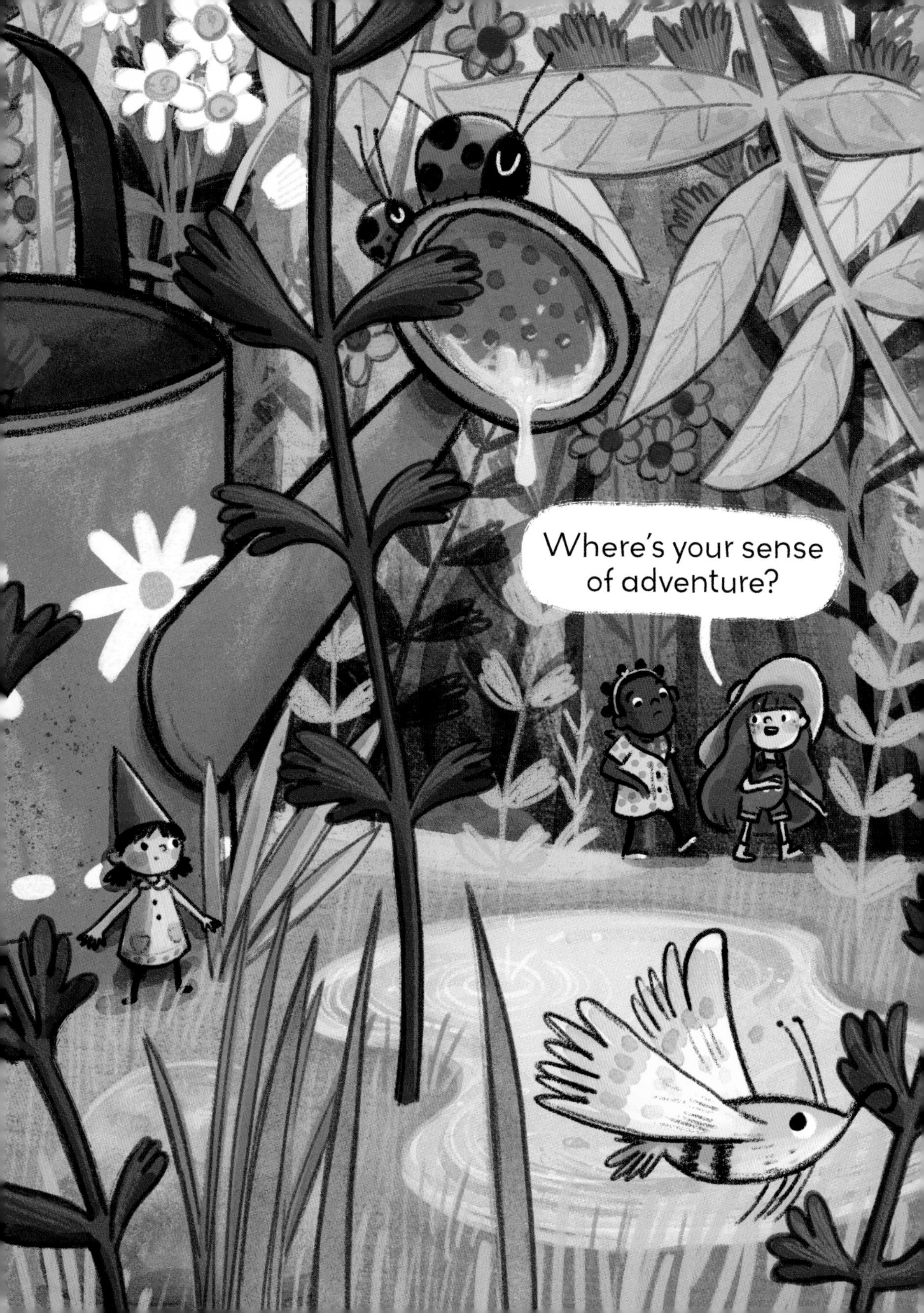
Where's your sense of adventure?

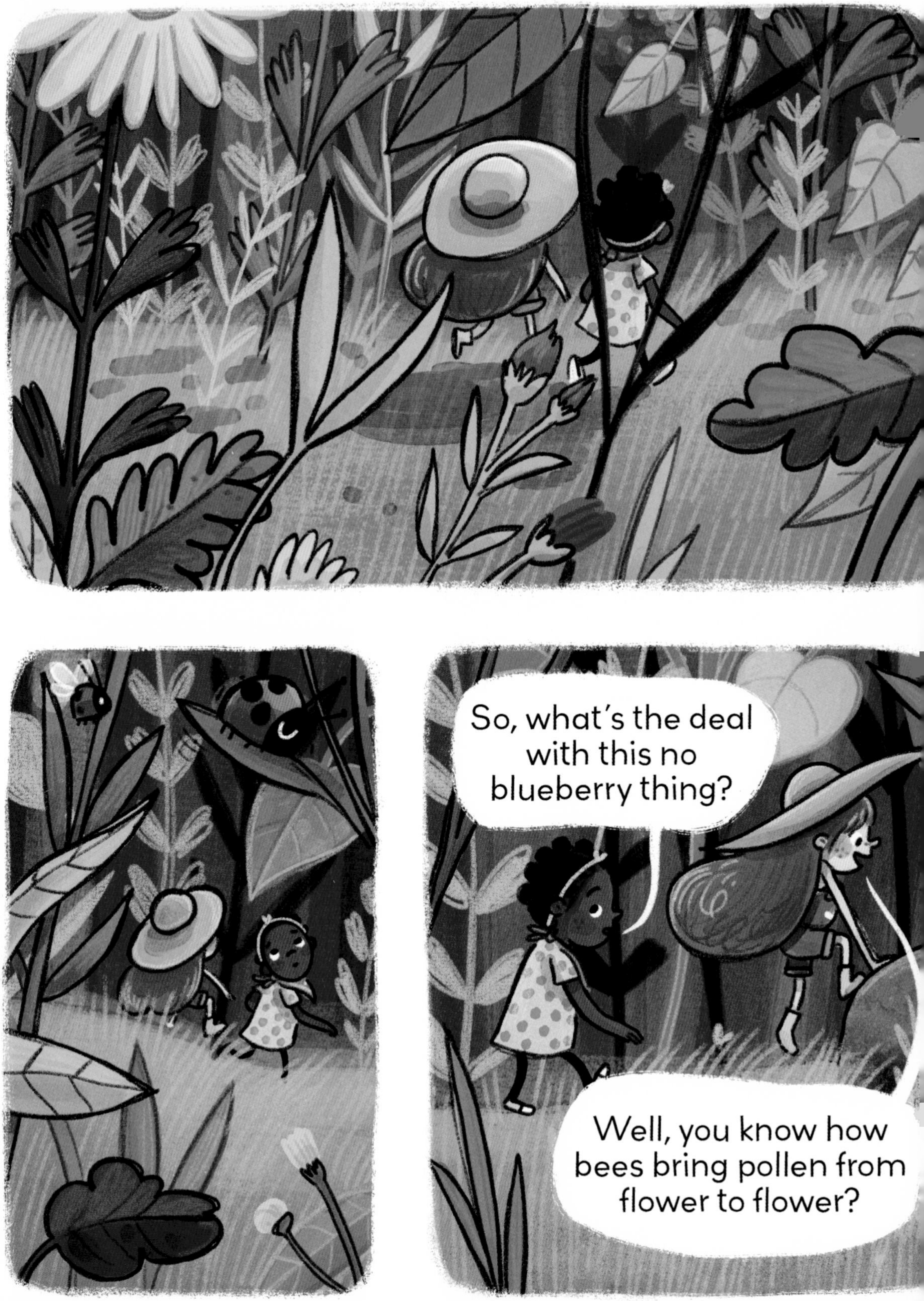
So, what's the deal with this no blueberry thing?
Well, you know how bees bring pollen from flower to flower?

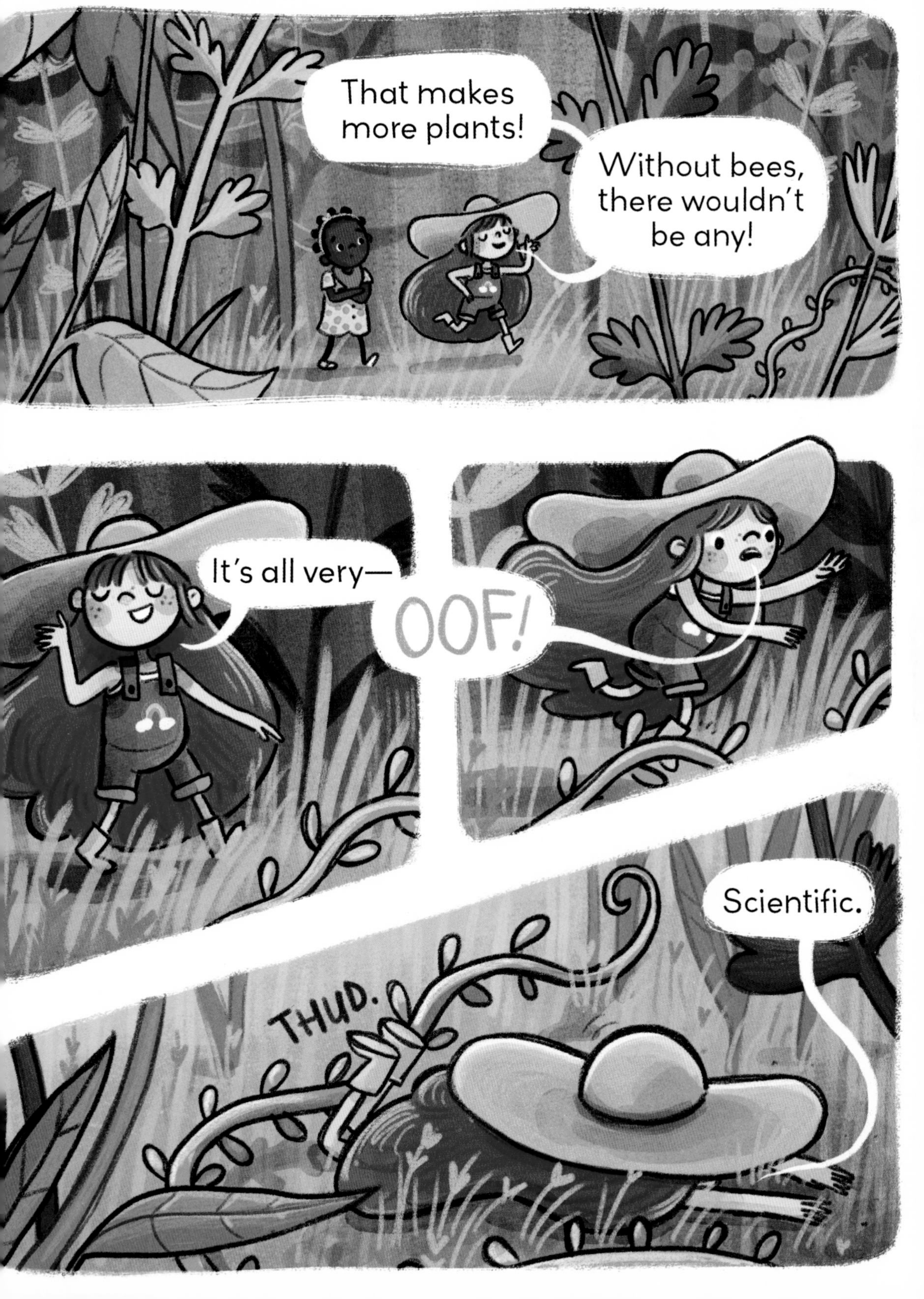
That makes more plants!
Without bees, there wouldn't be any!
It's all very—
OOF!
THUD.
Scientific.

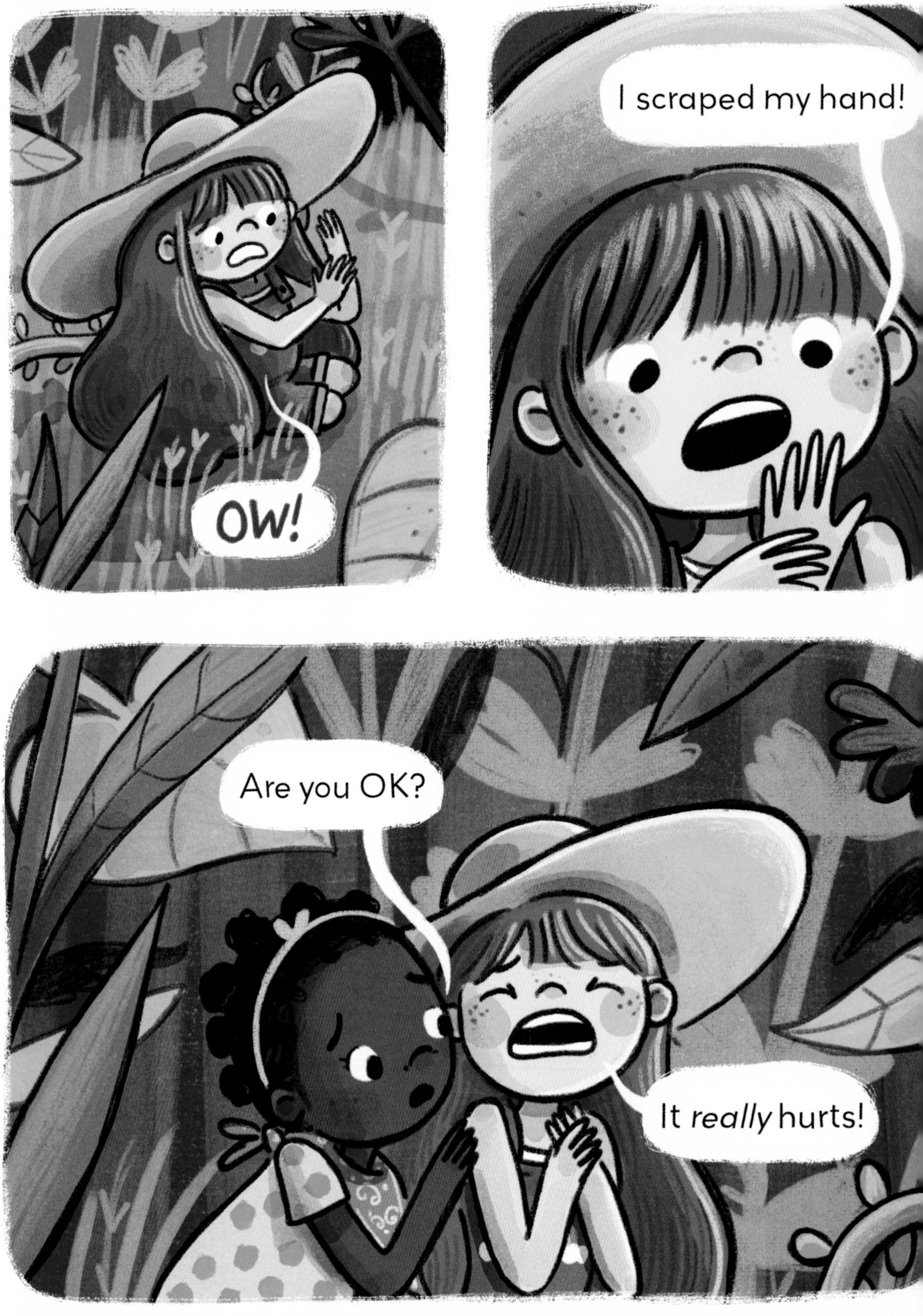
OW!
I scraped my hand!
Are you OK?
It *really* hurts!

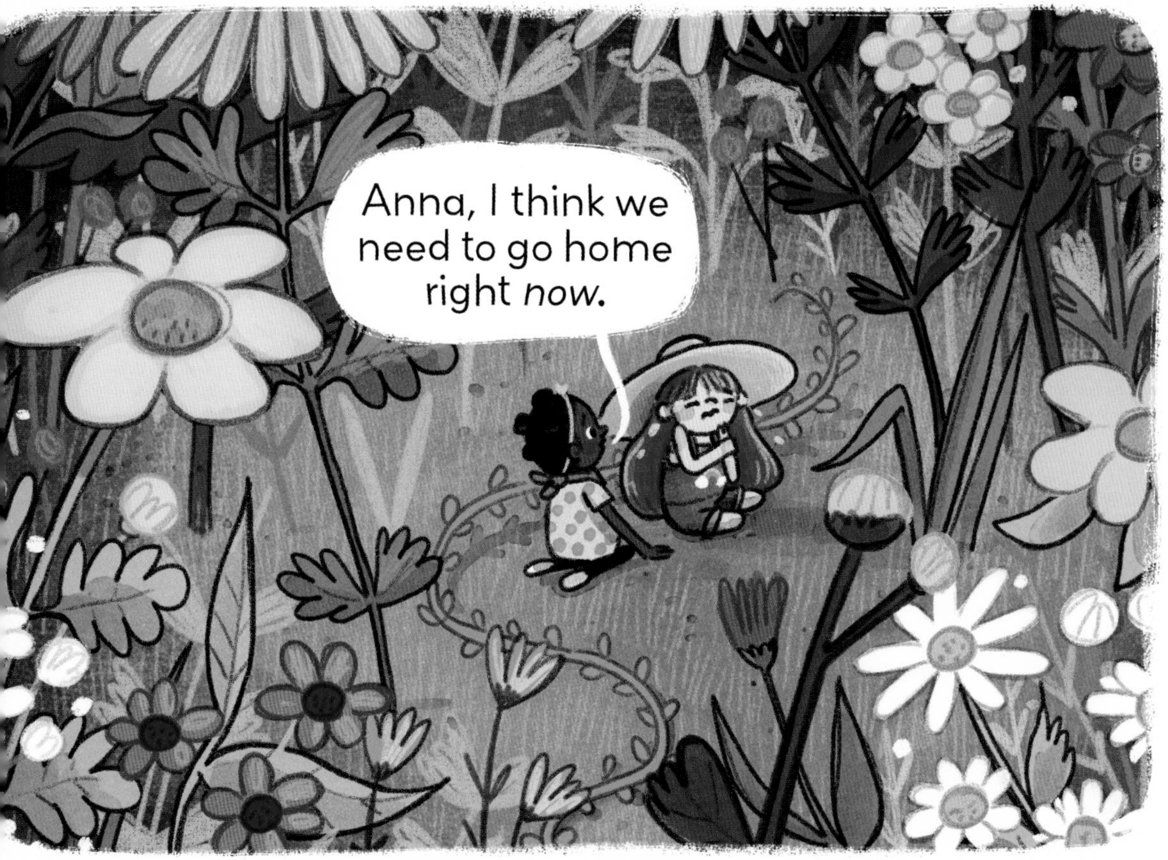
Anna, I think we need to go home right *now*.

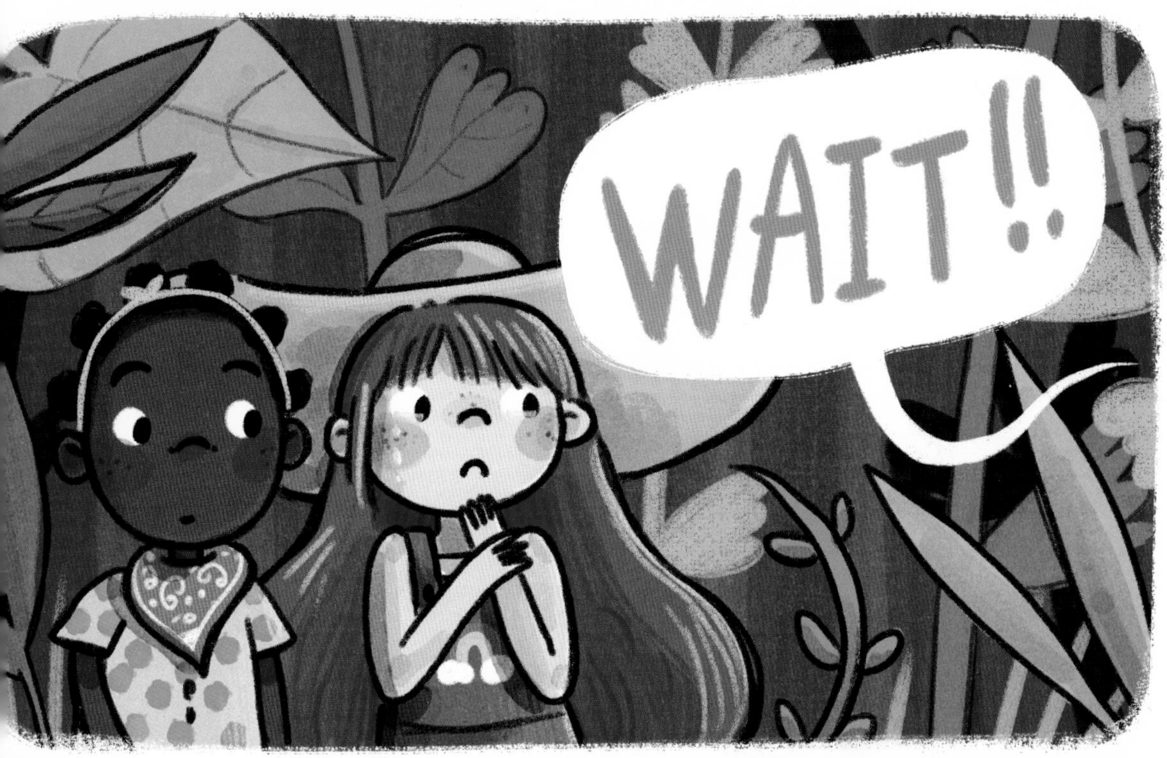
WAIT!!

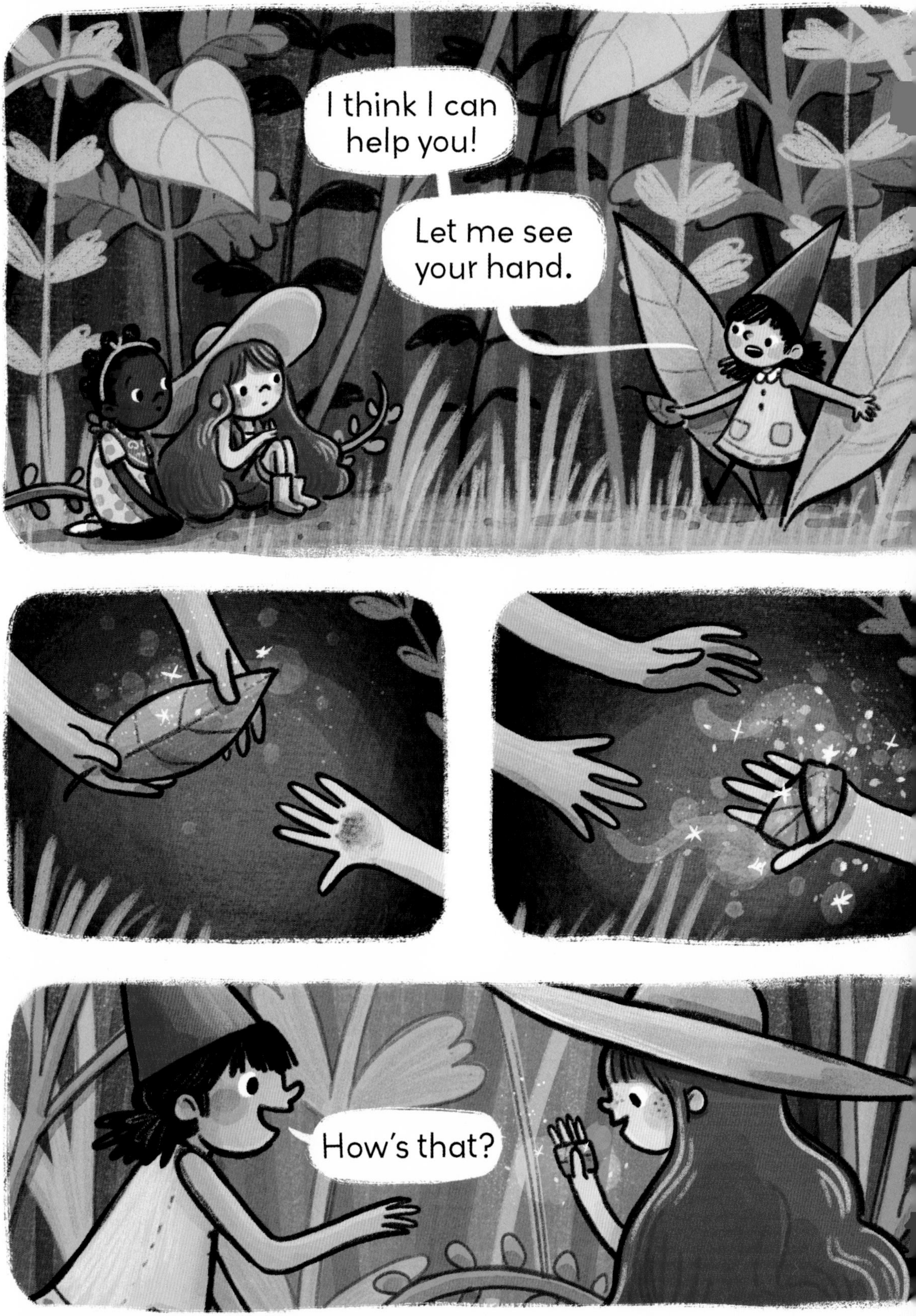
I think I can help you!
Let me see your hand.
How's that?

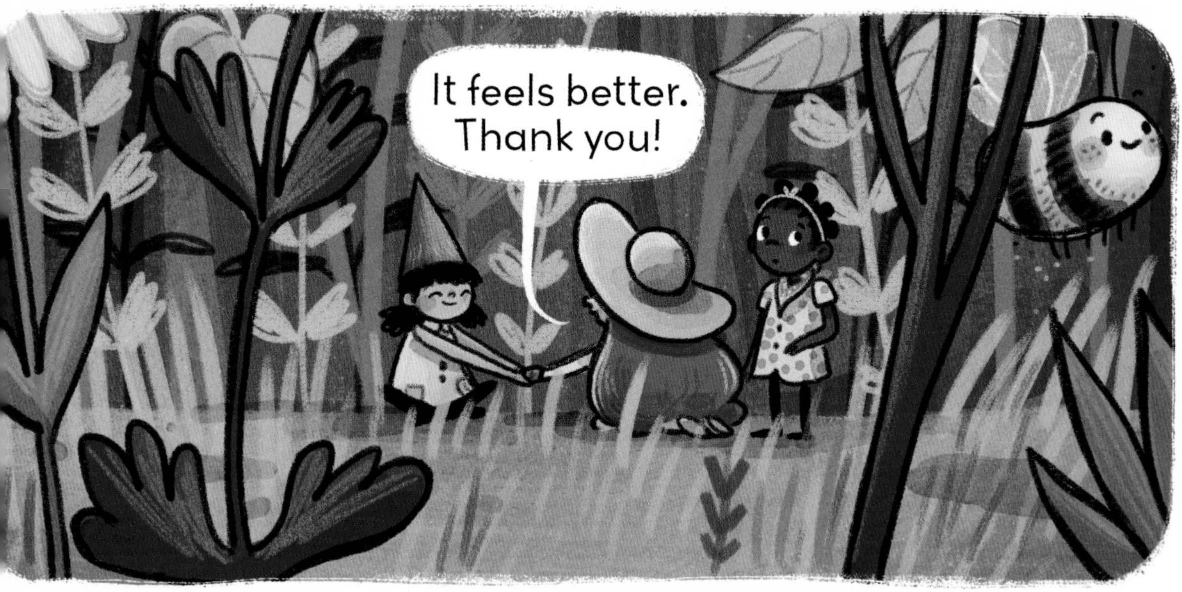
It feels better. Thank you!

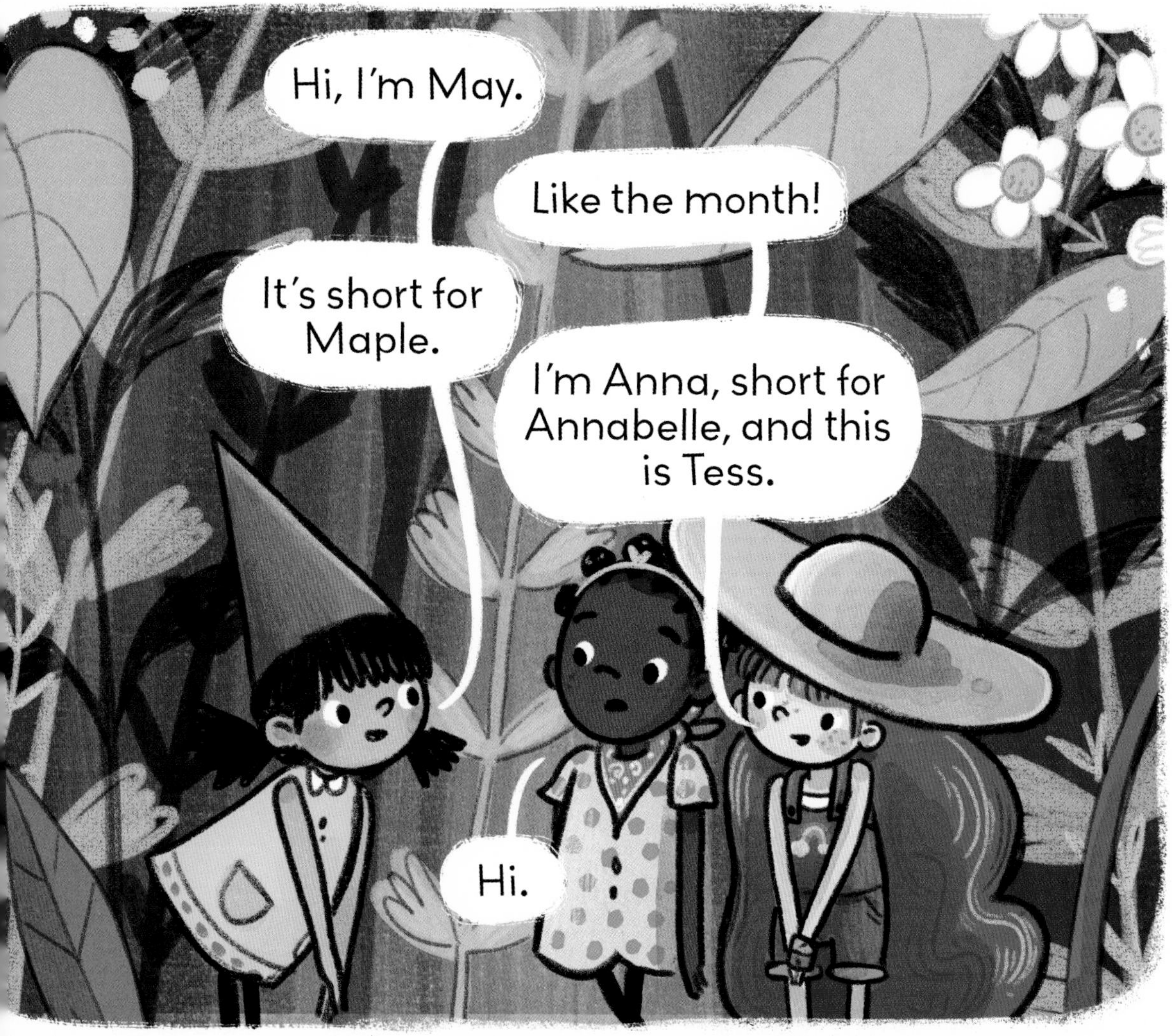
Hi, I'm May.
Like the month!
It's short for Maple.
I'm Anna, short for Annabelle, and this is Tess.
Hi.

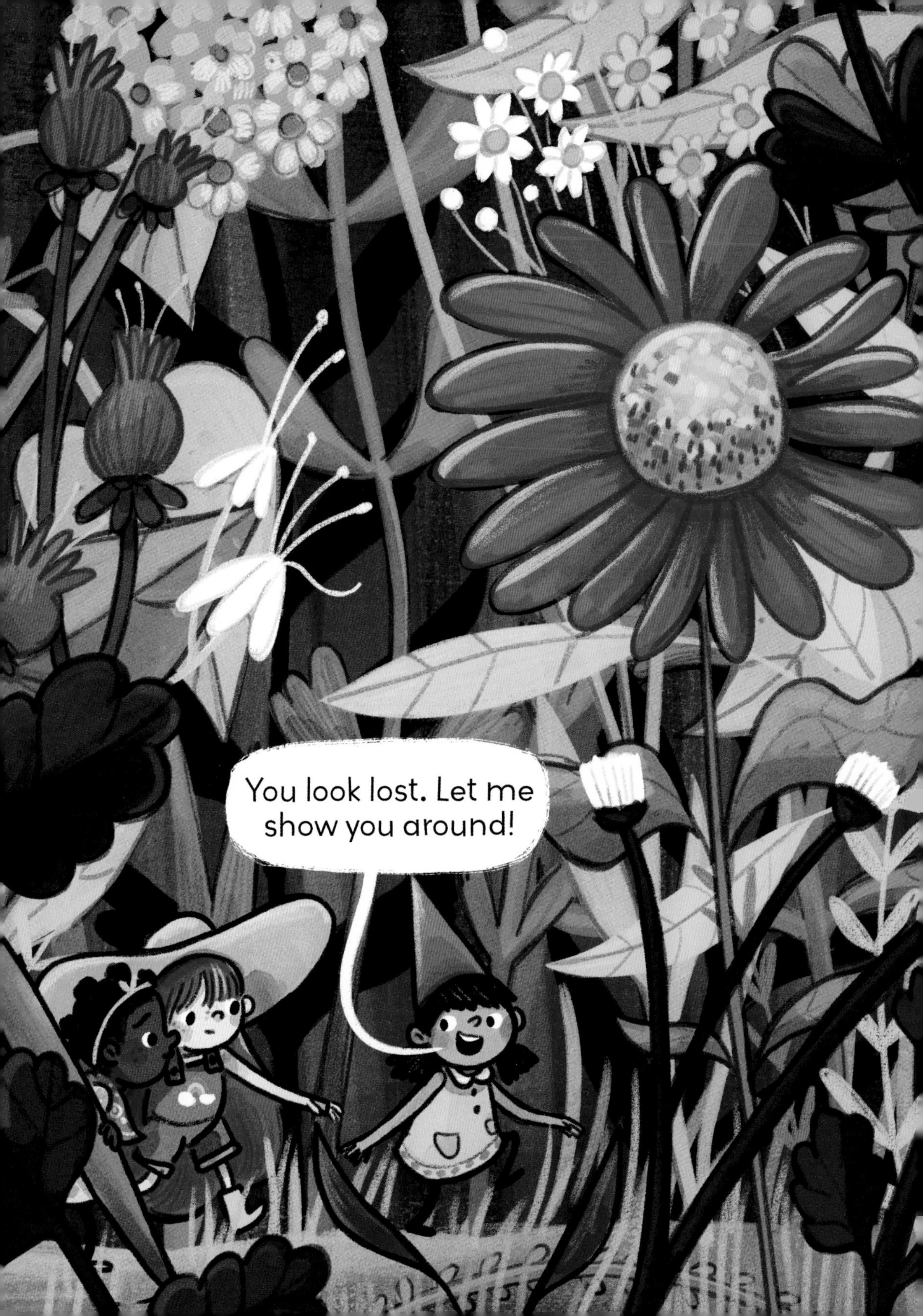
You look lost. Let me show you around!

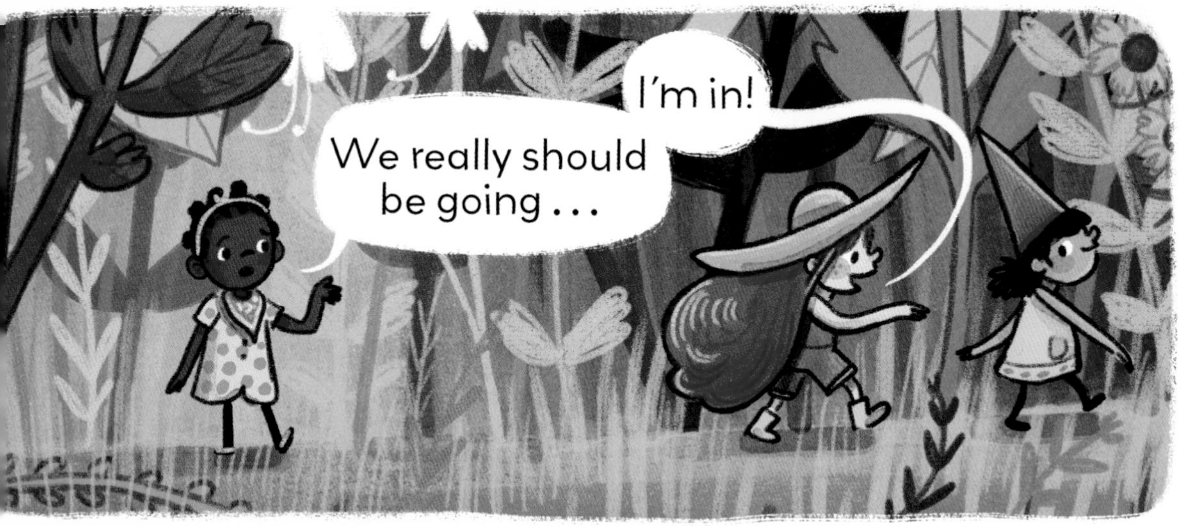
We really should be going . . .
I'm in!

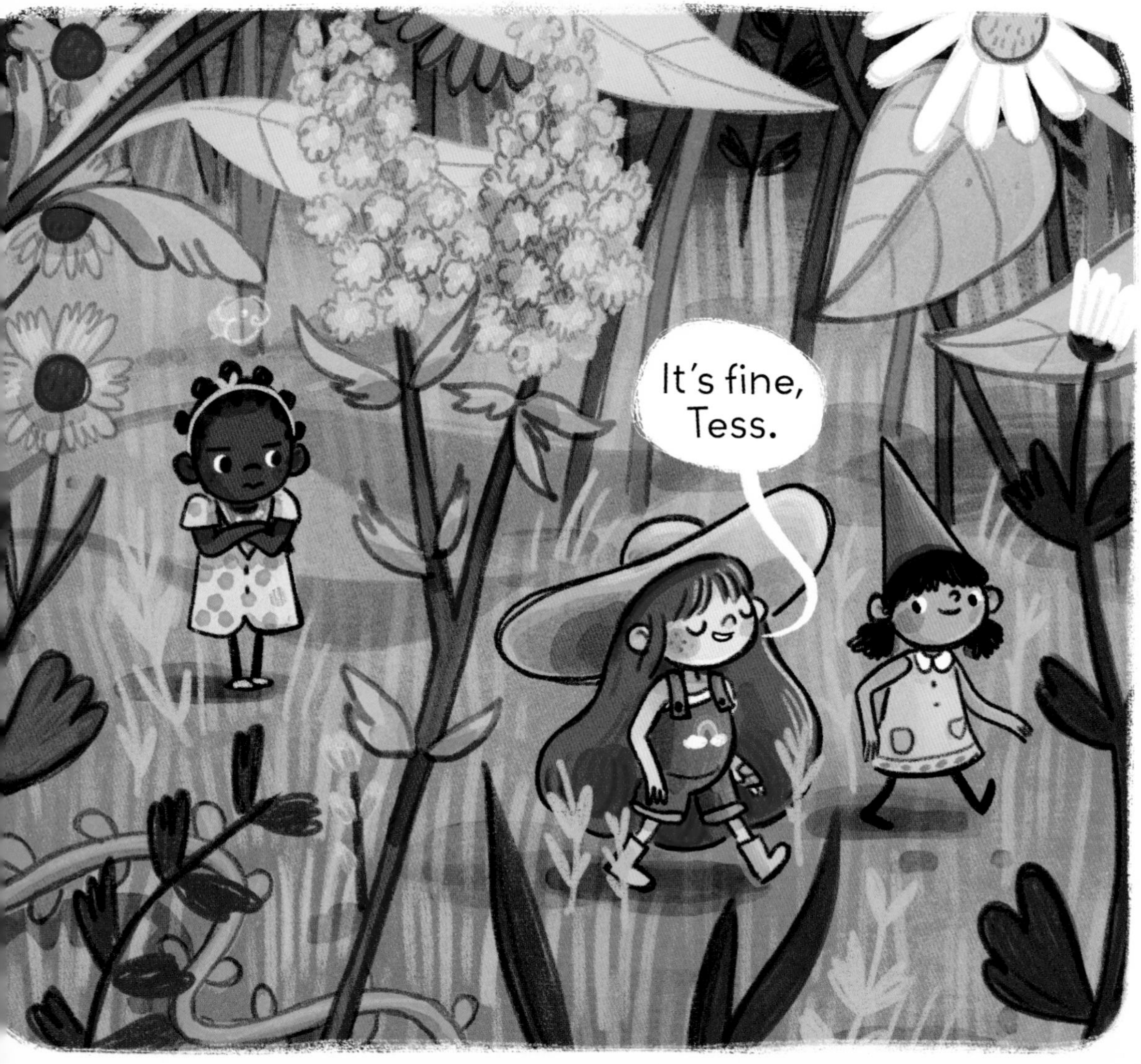
It's fine, Tess.

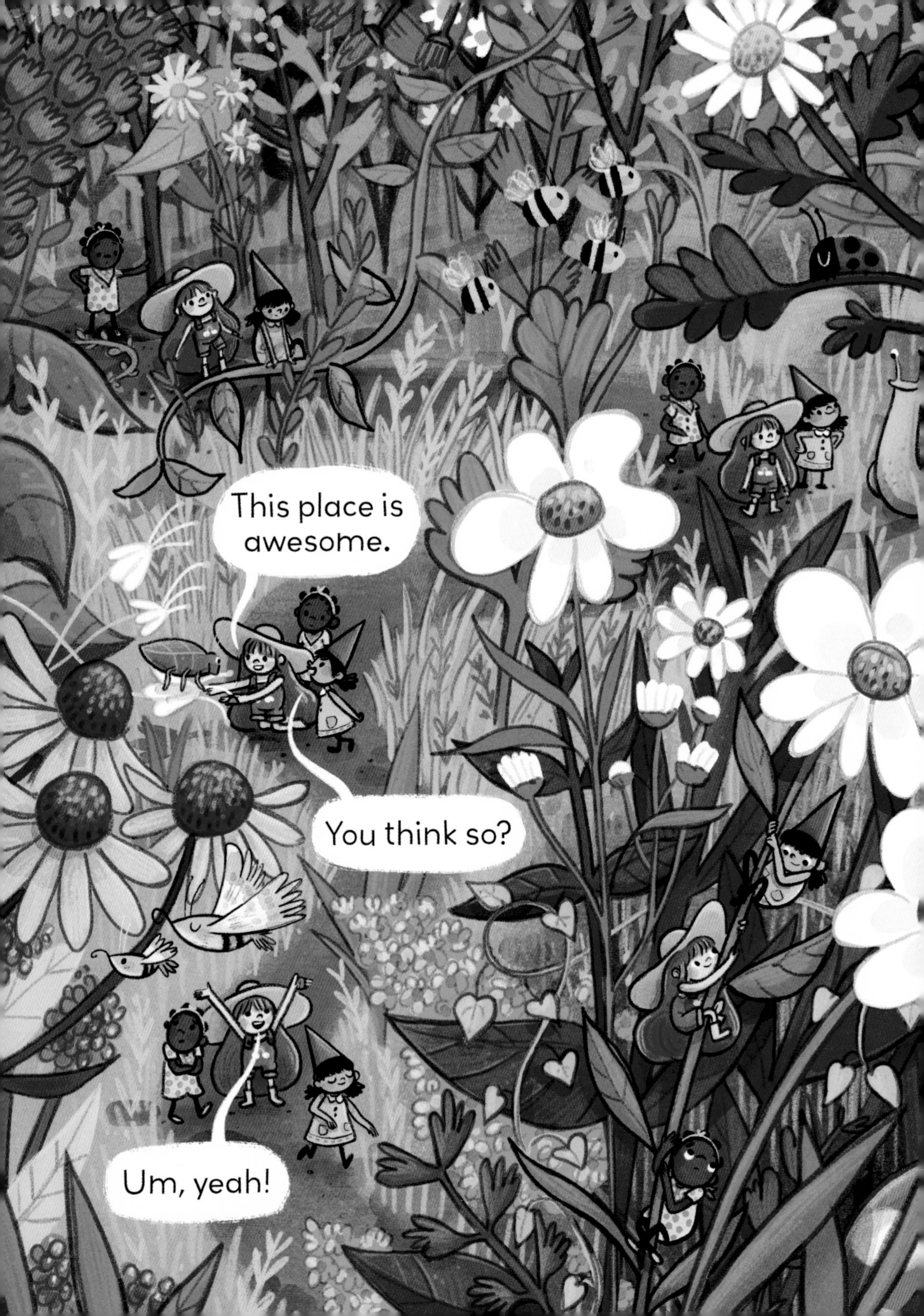
This place is awesome.
You think so?
Um, yeah!

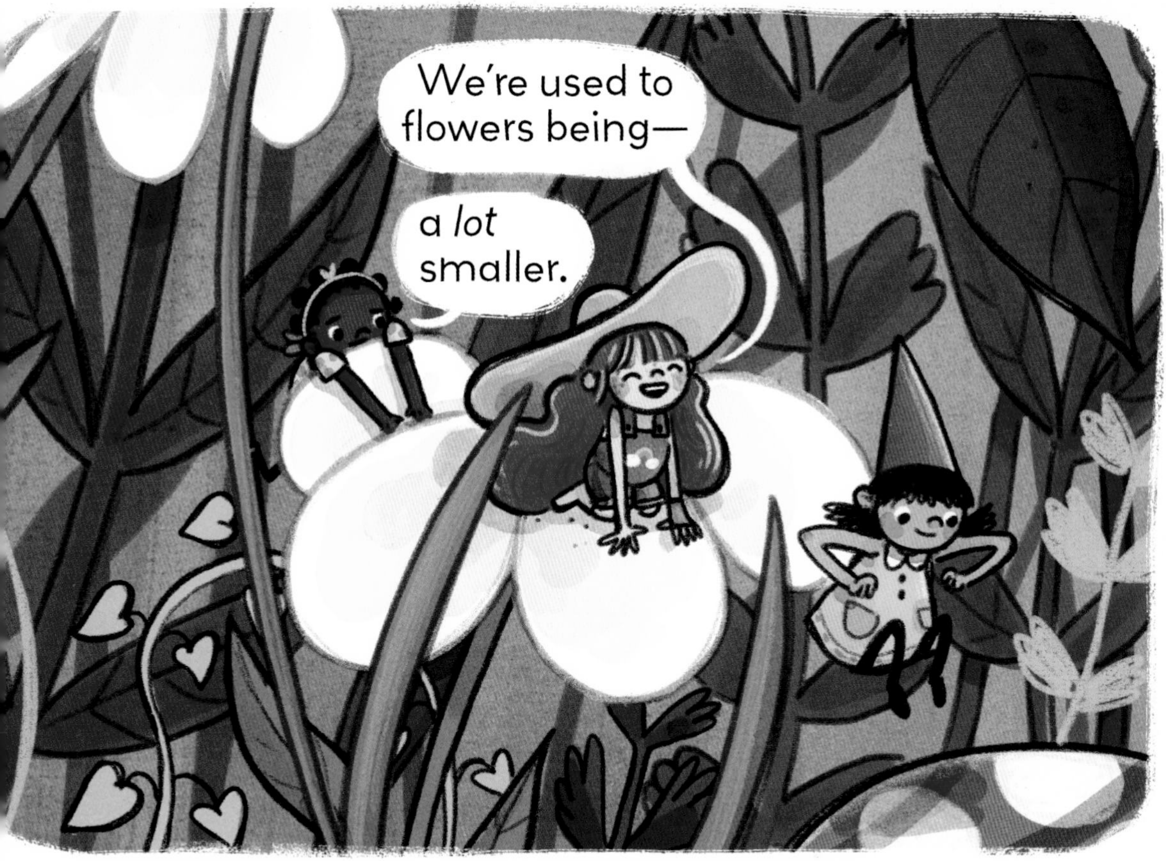
We're used to flowers being—
a *lot* smaller.

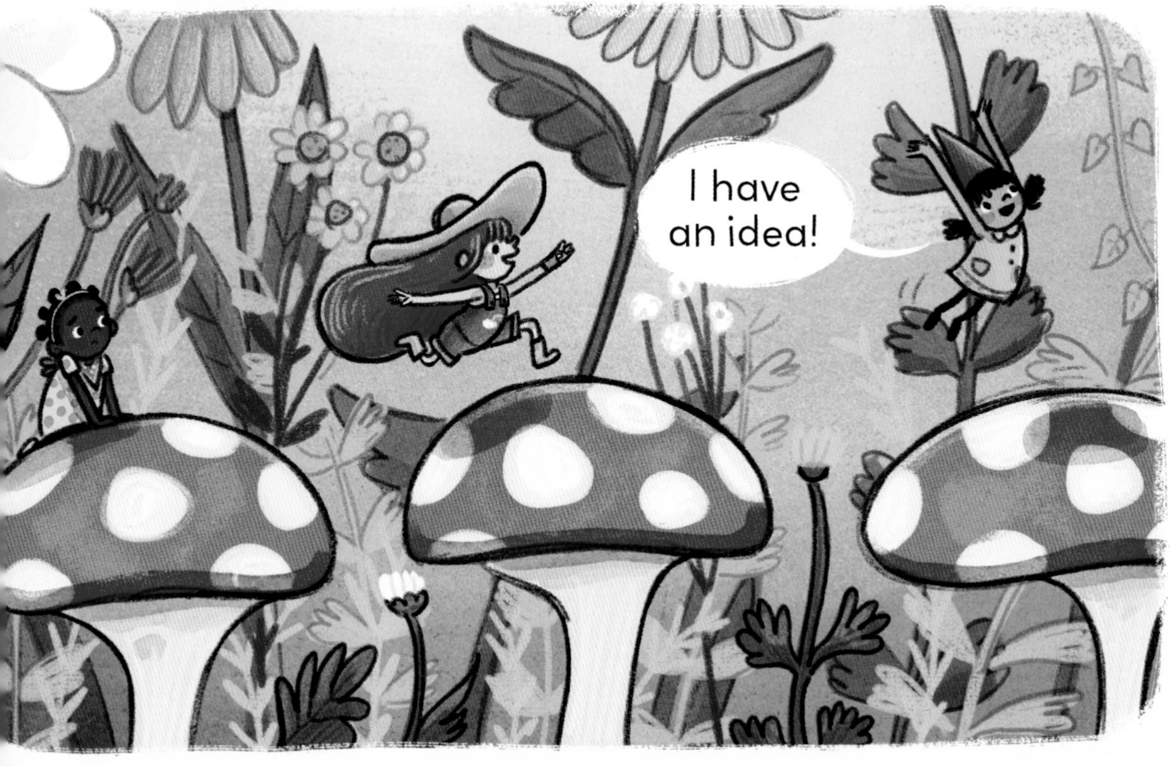
I have an idea!

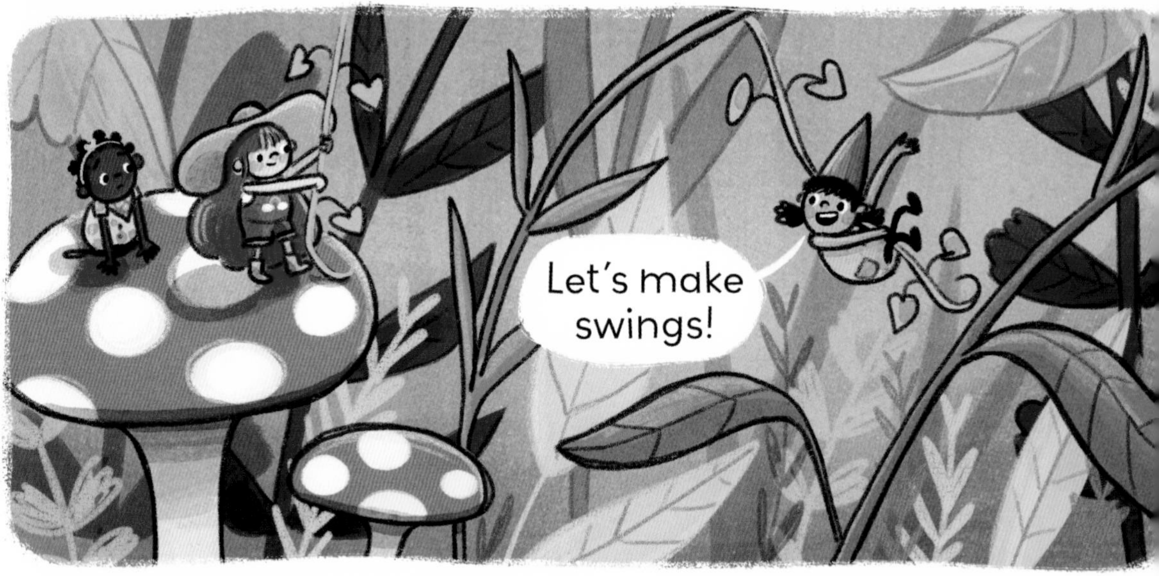
Let's make swings!
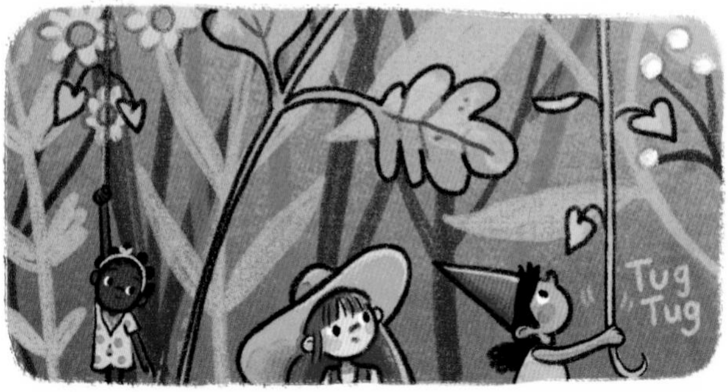
Tug Tug
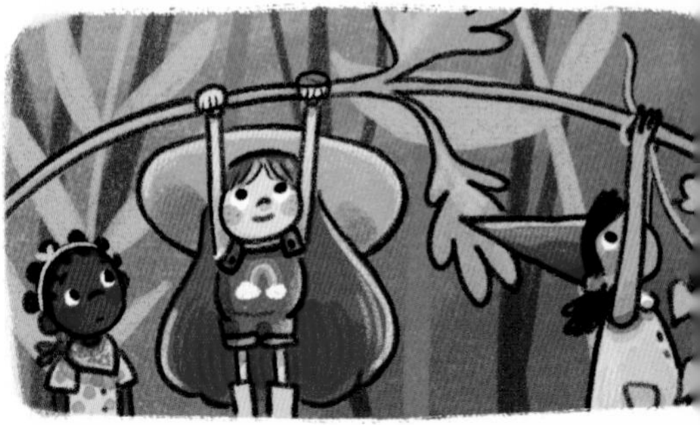
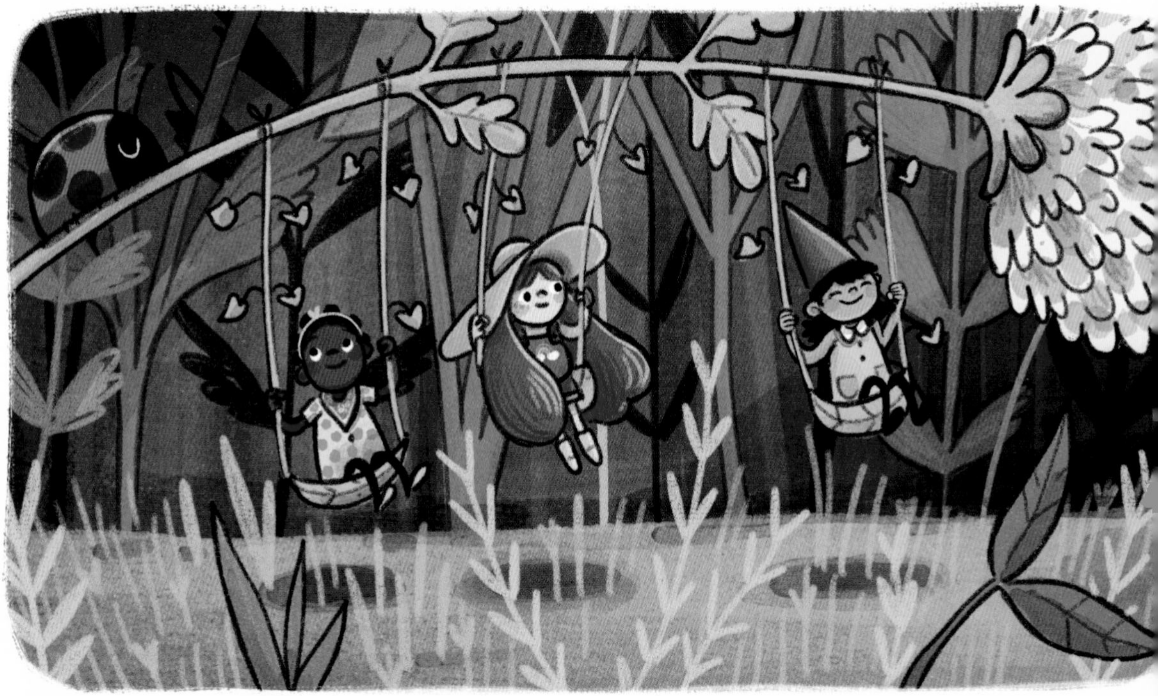

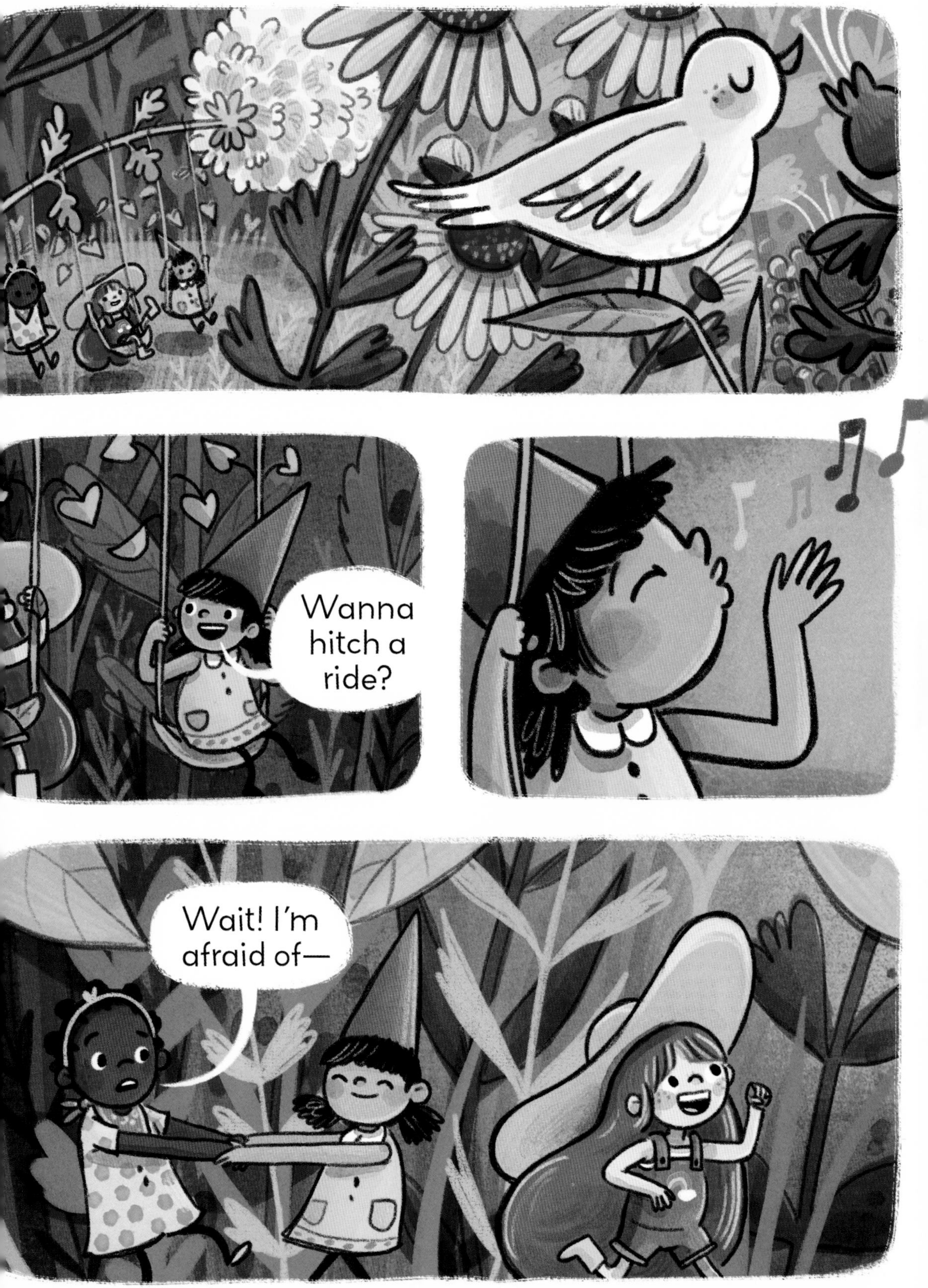
Wanna hitch a ride?
Wait! I'm afraid of—

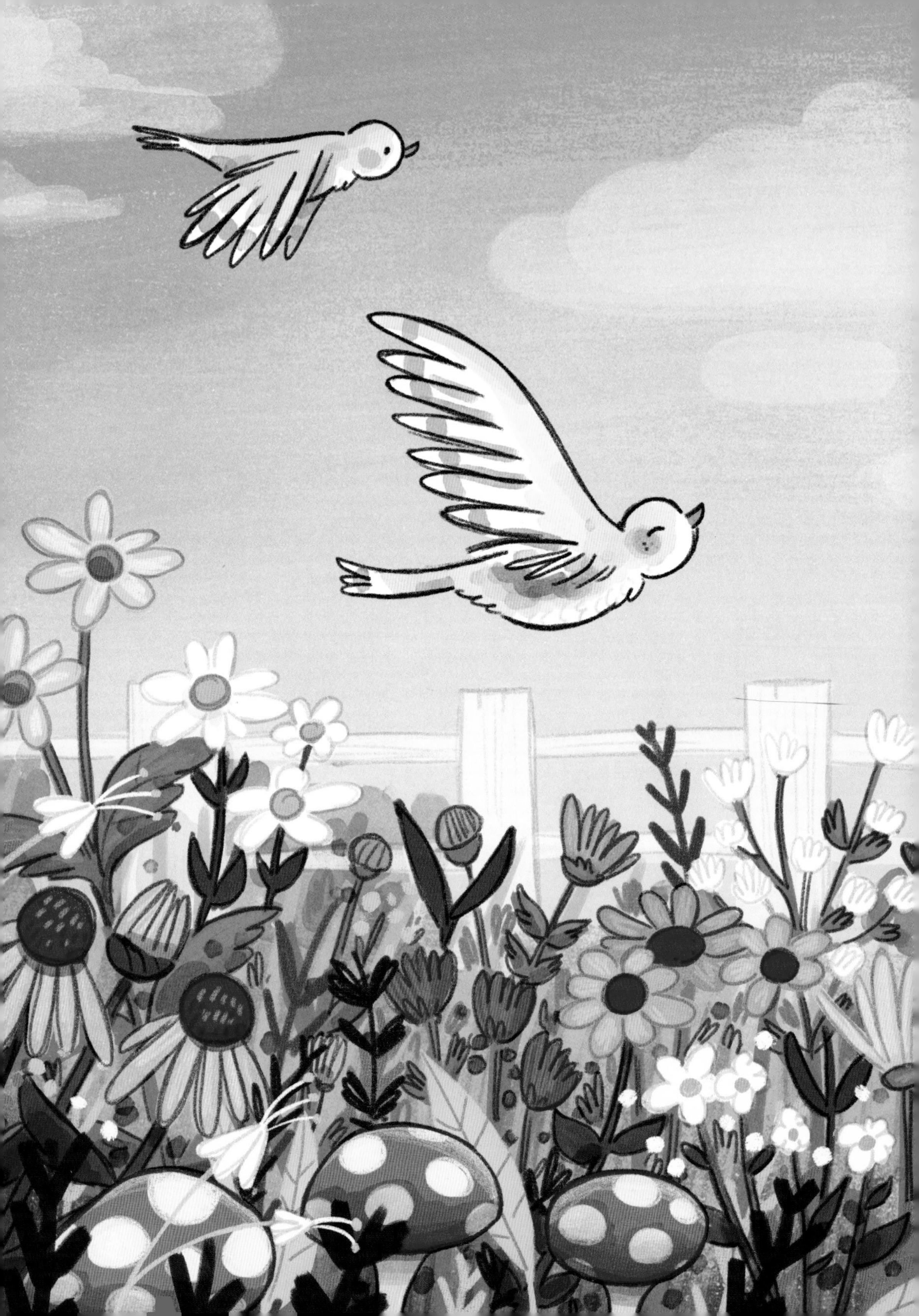

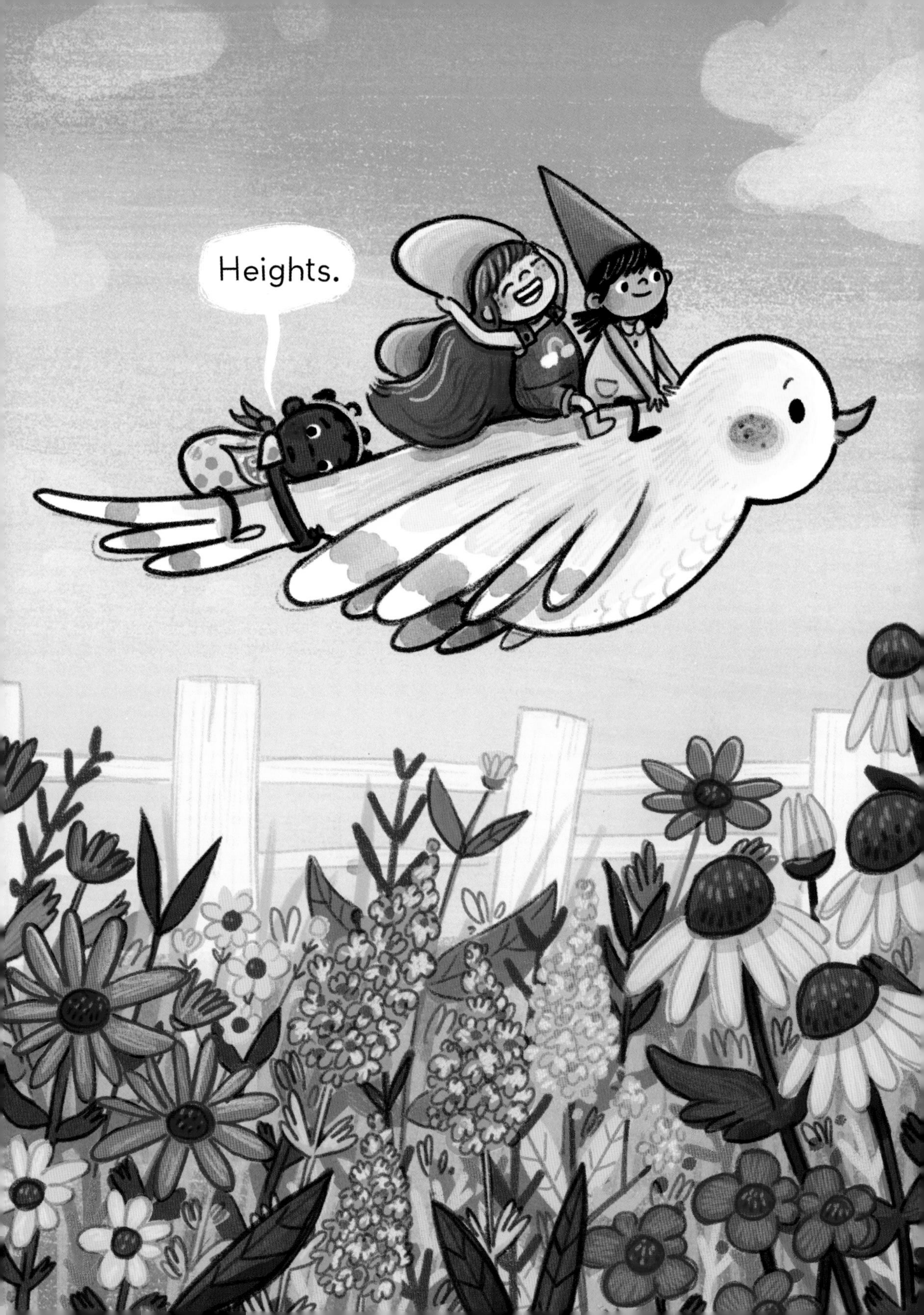
Heights.

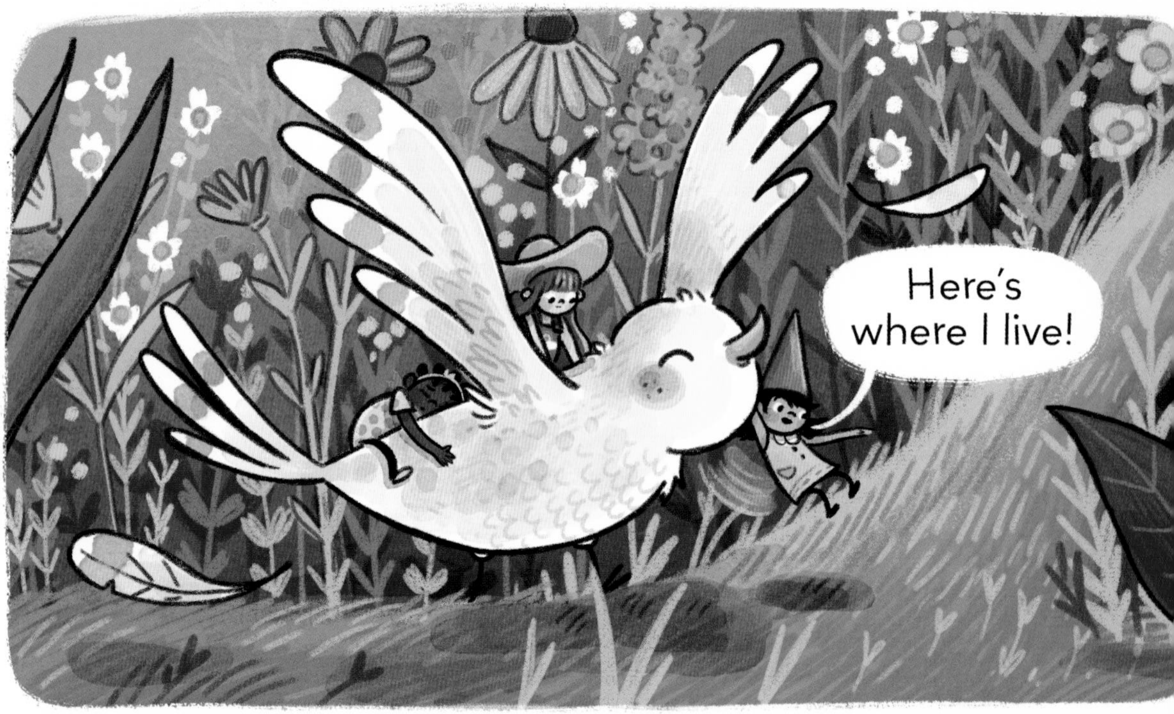
Here's where I live!

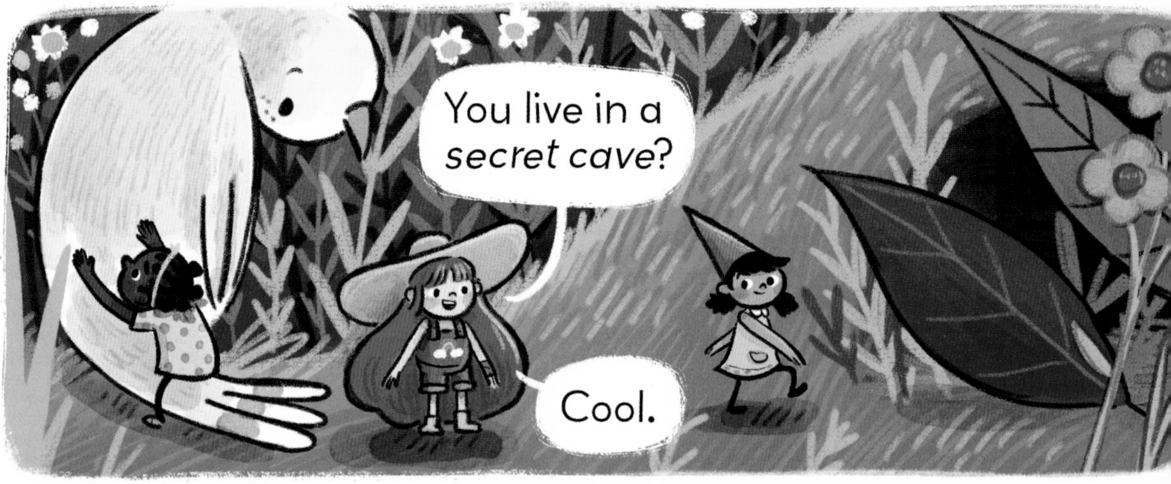
You live in a *secret cave*?
Cool.

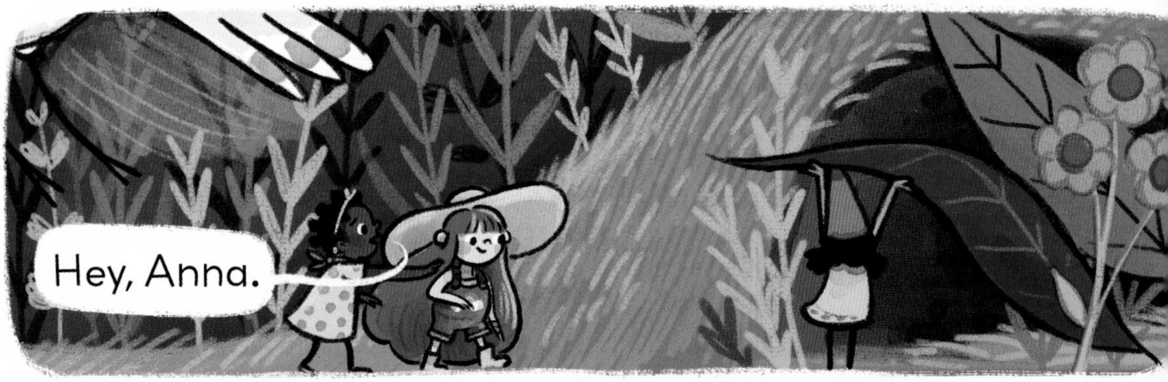
Hey, Anna.

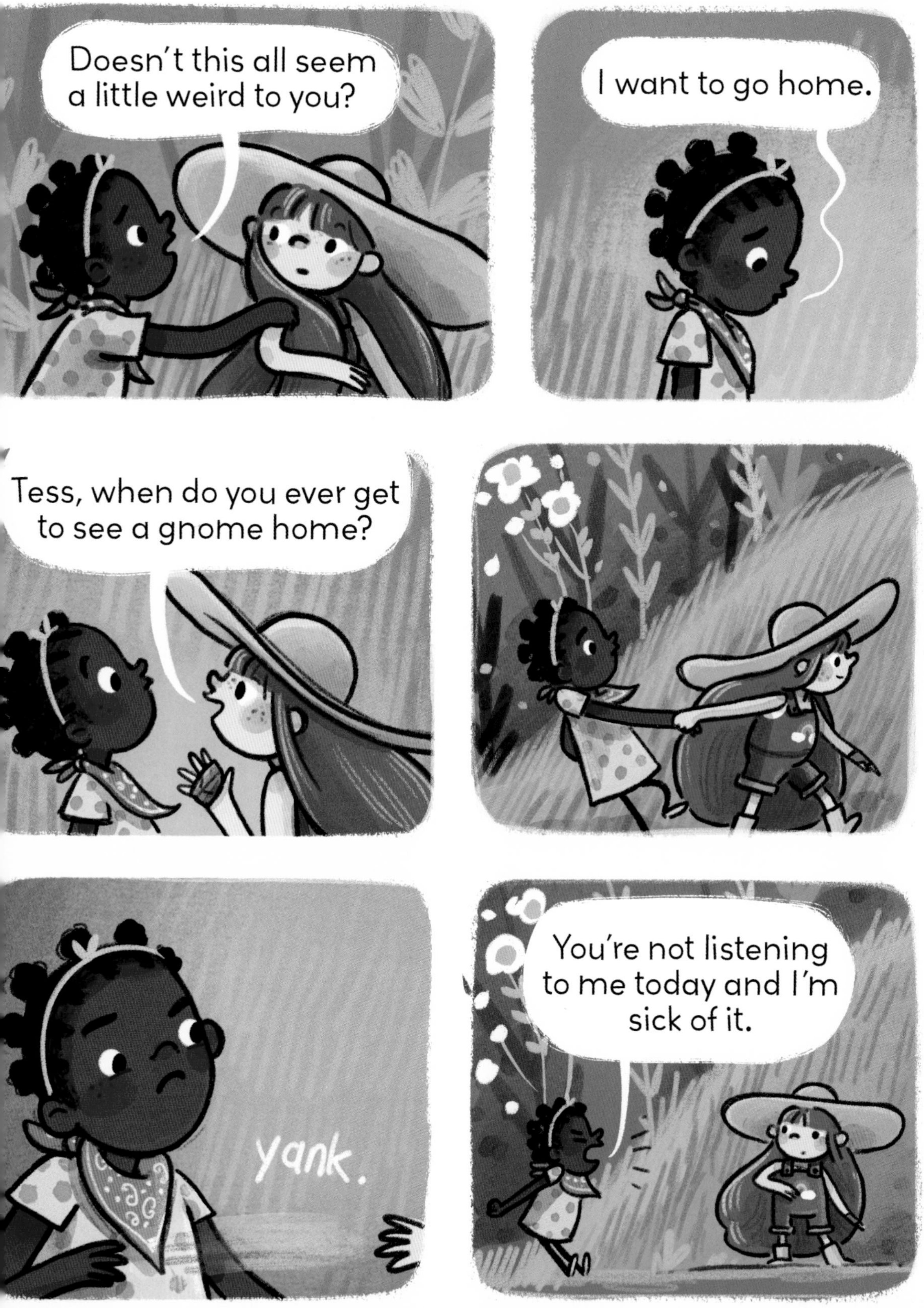

Doesn't this all seem a little weird to you?
I want to go home.
Tess, when do you ever get to see a gnome home?
yank.
You're not listening to me today and I'm sick of it.

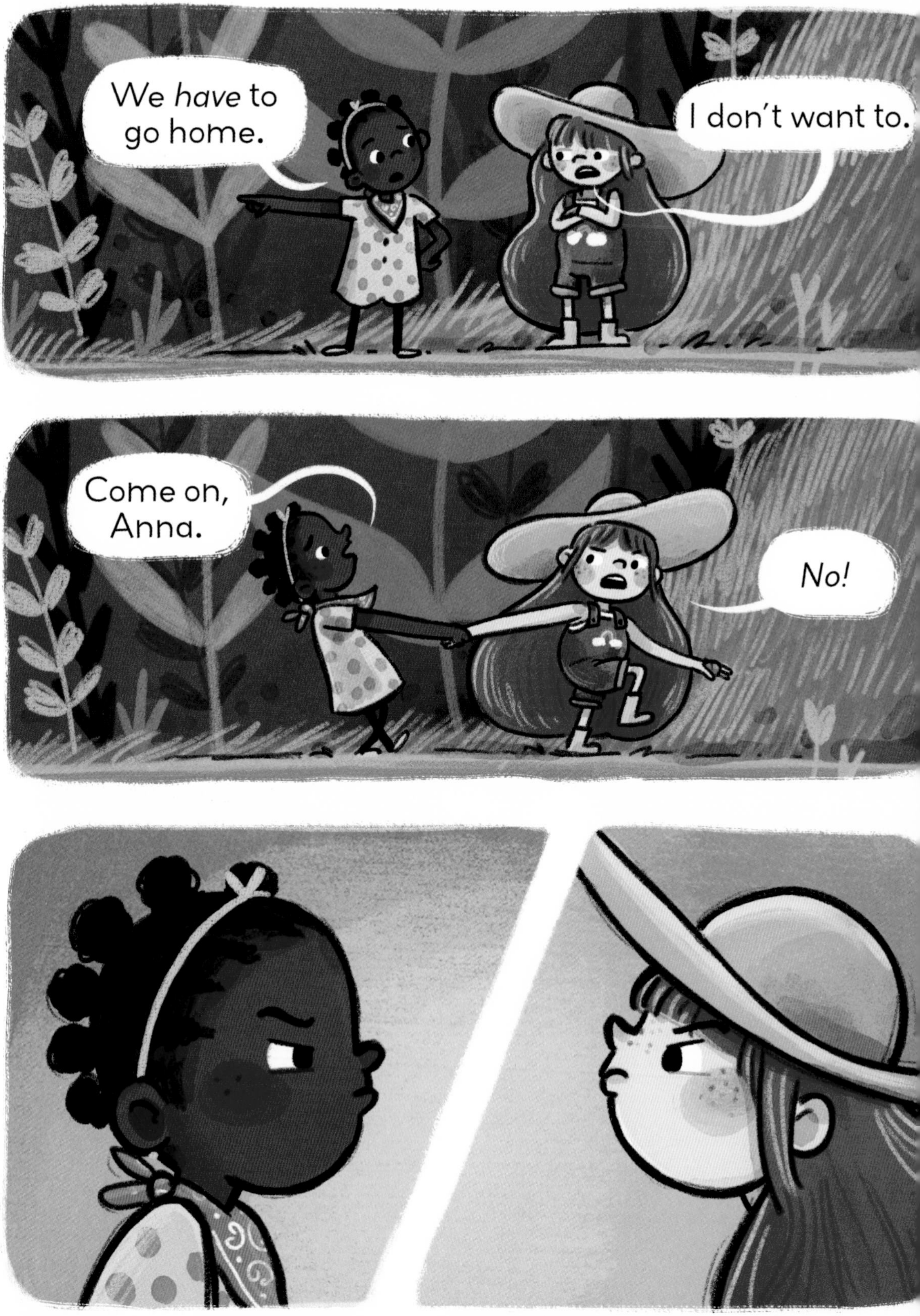
We *have* to go home.
I don't want to.
Come on, Anna.
No!

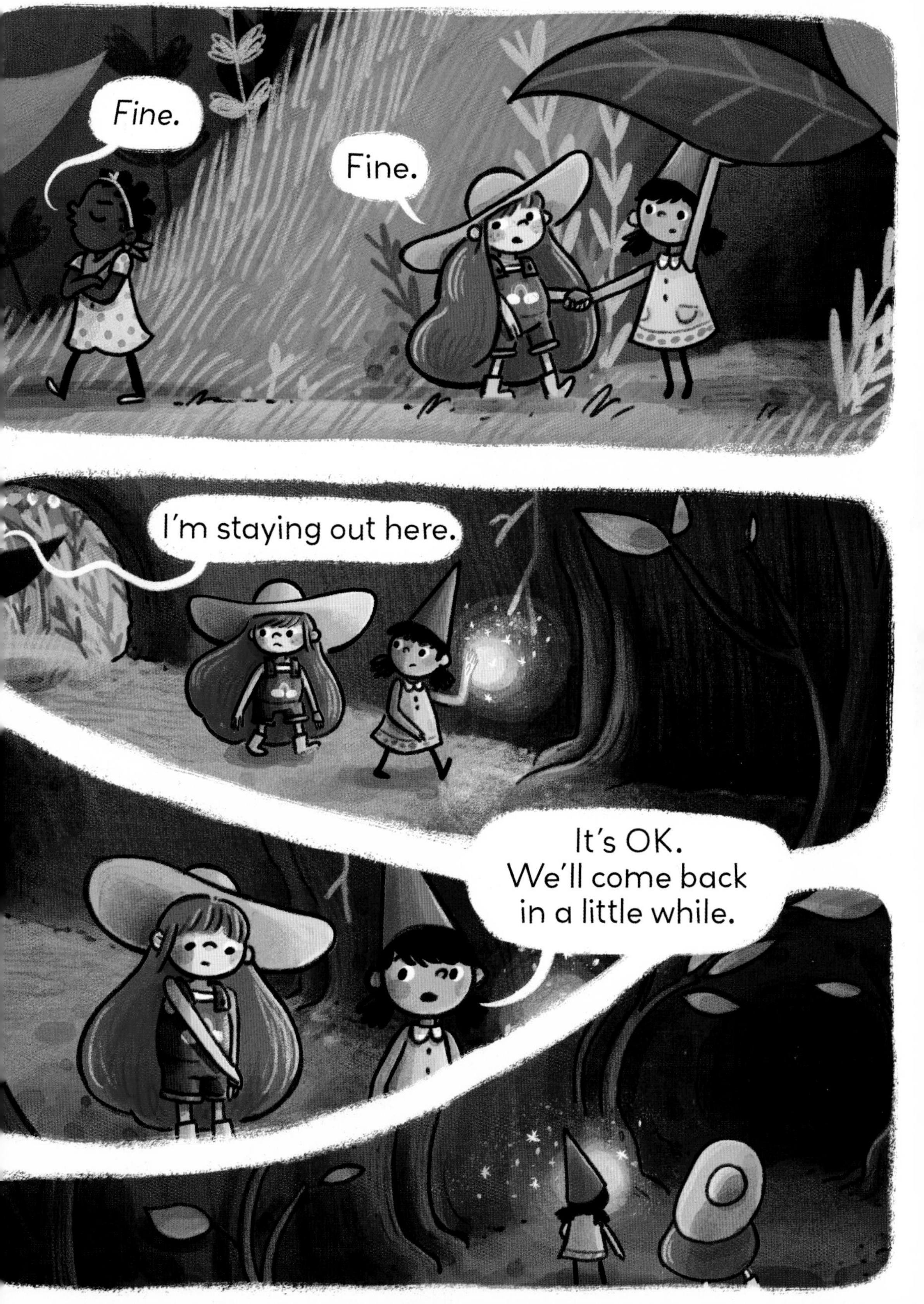
Fine.
Fine.
I'm staying out here.
It's OK. We'll come back in a little while.

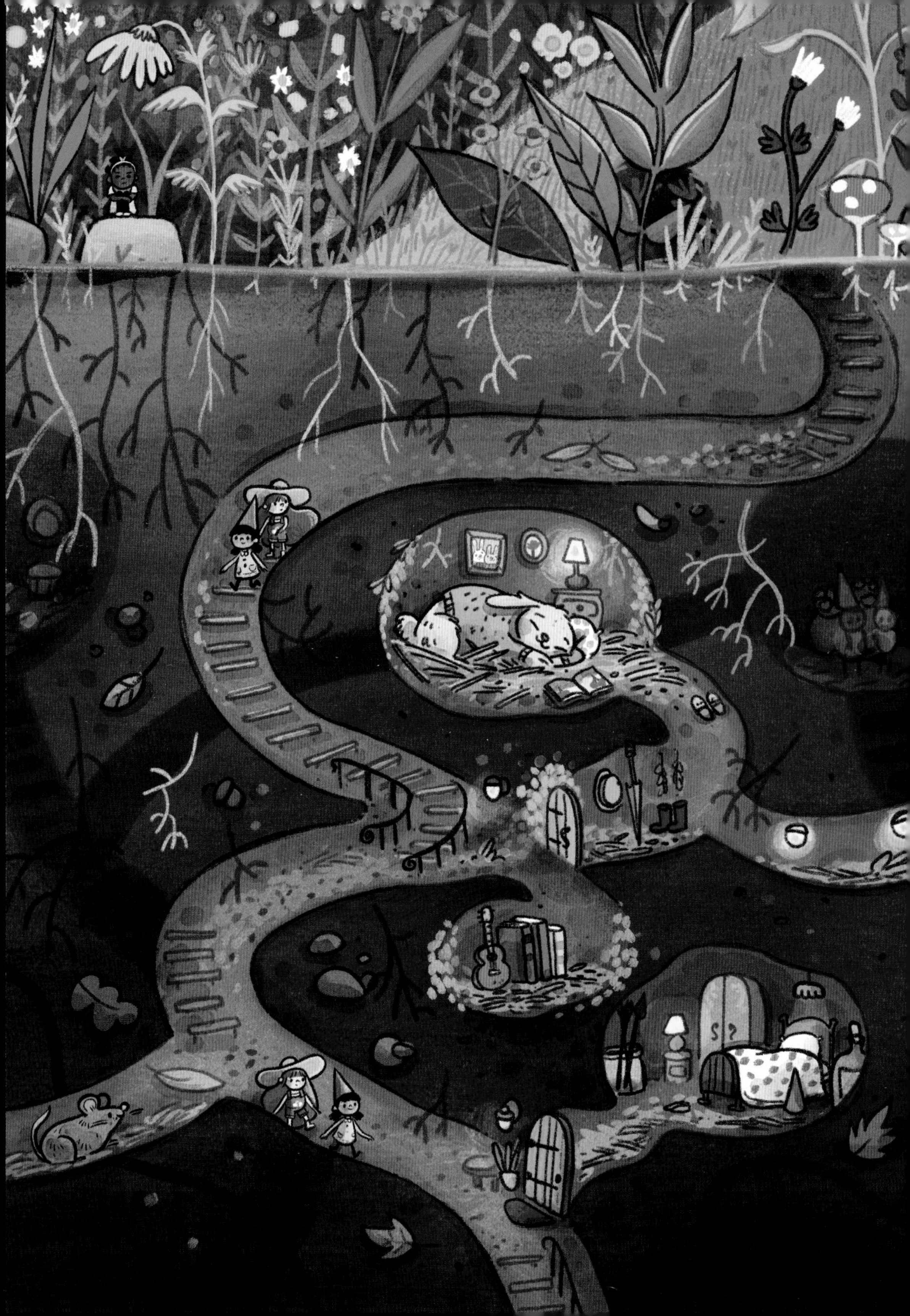

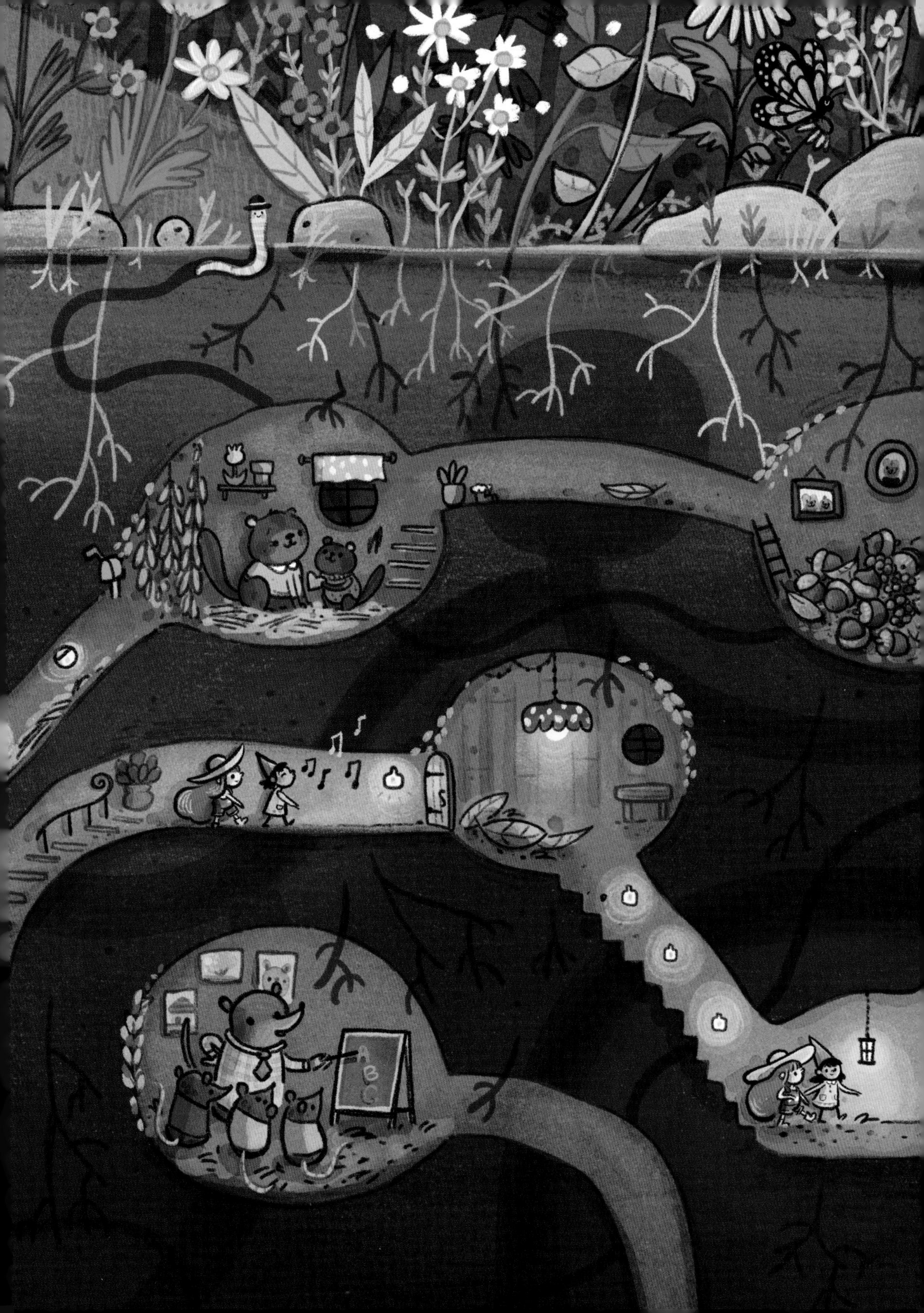

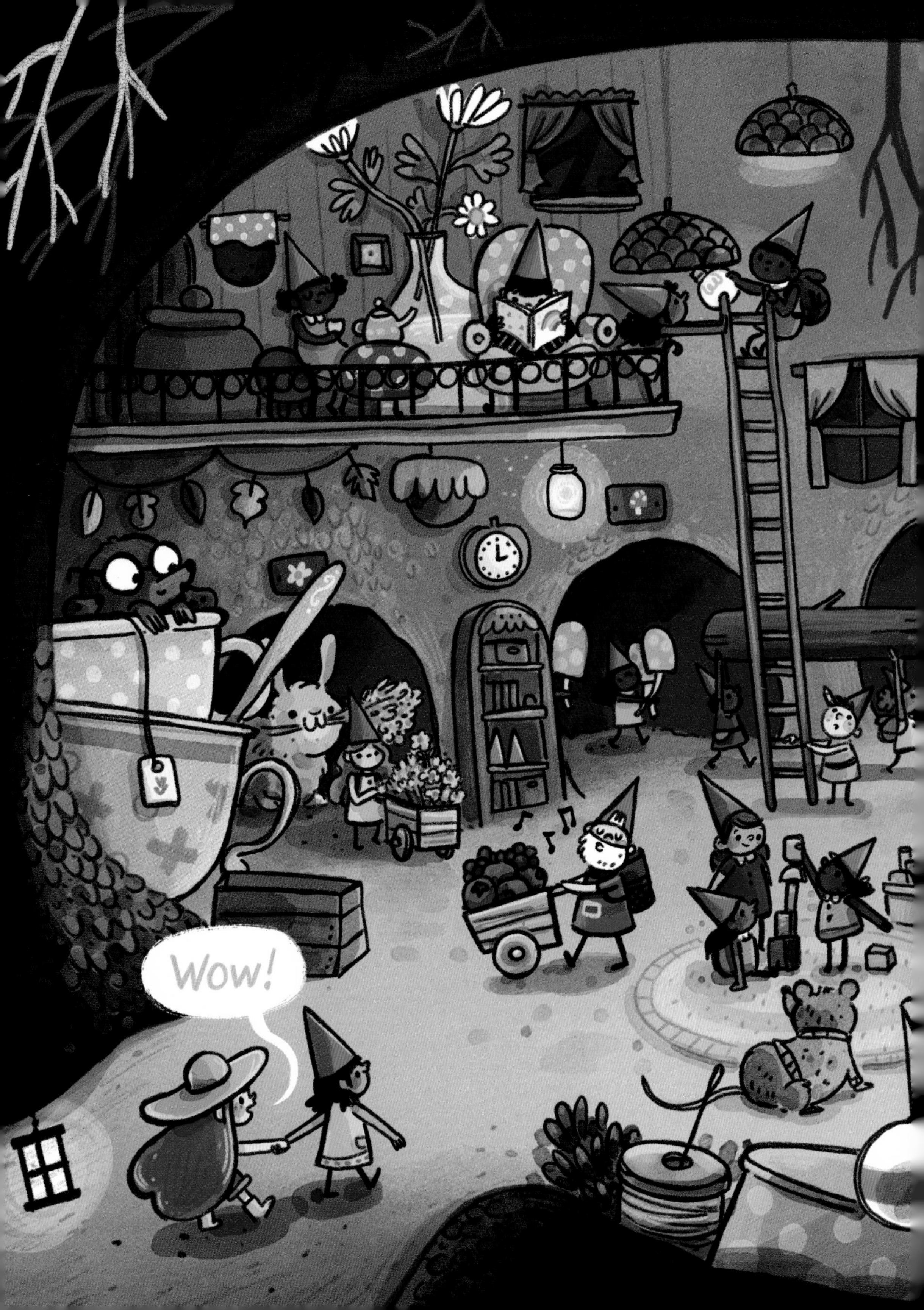
Wow!

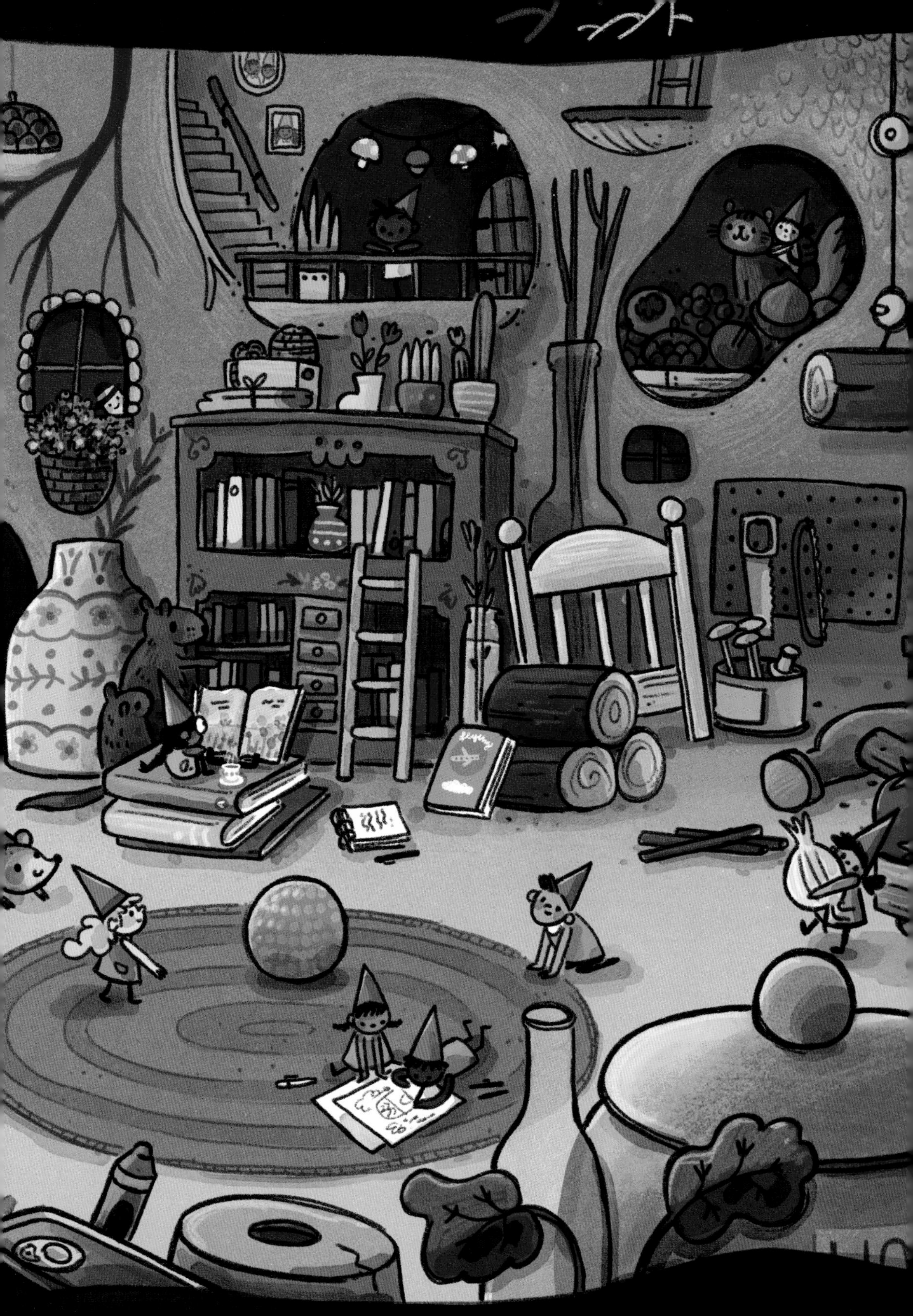

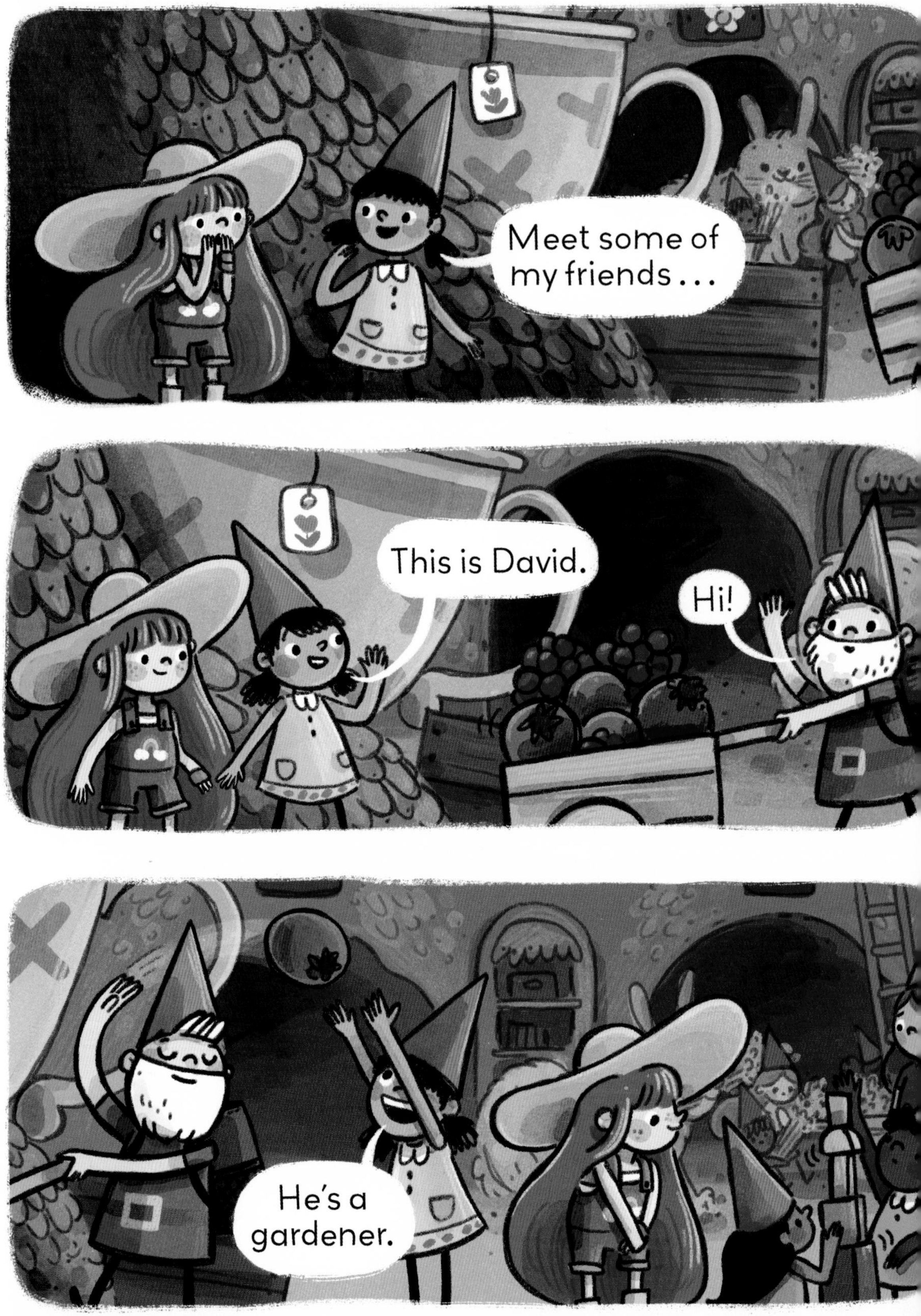
Meet some of my friends . . .
This is David.
Hi!
He's a gardener.

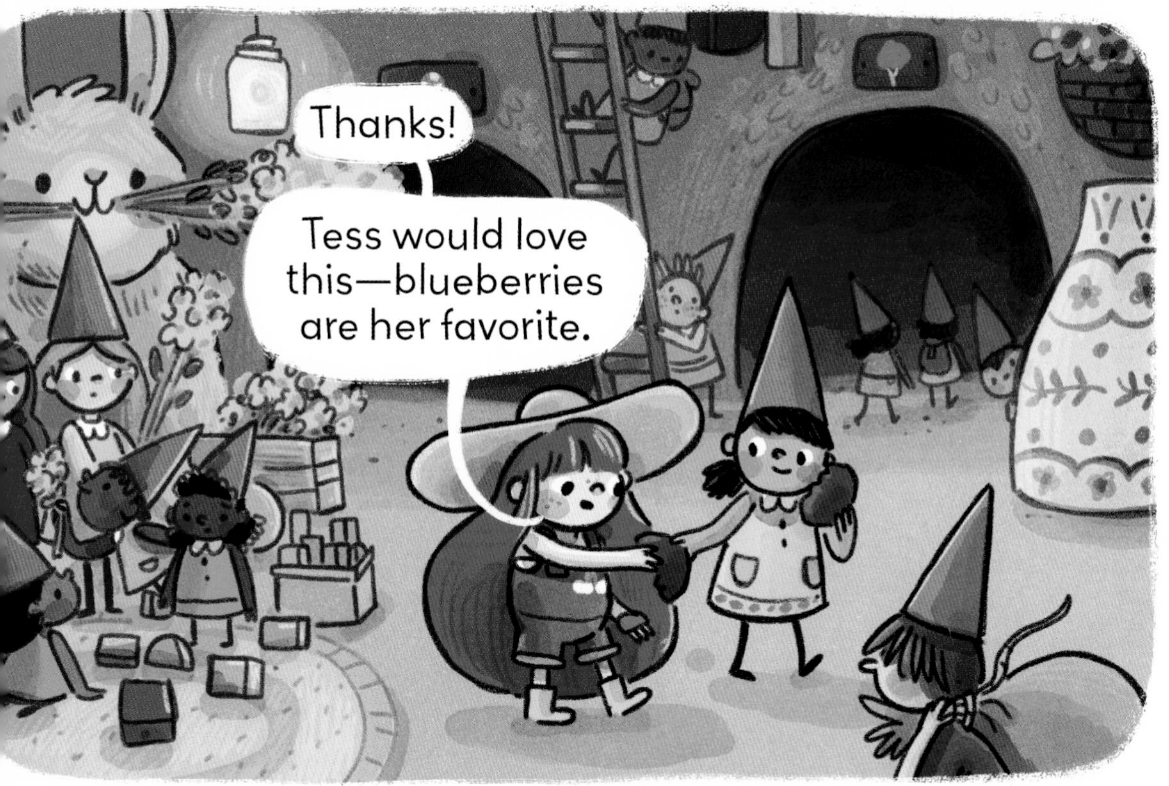
Thanks!
Tess would love this—blueberries are her favorite.

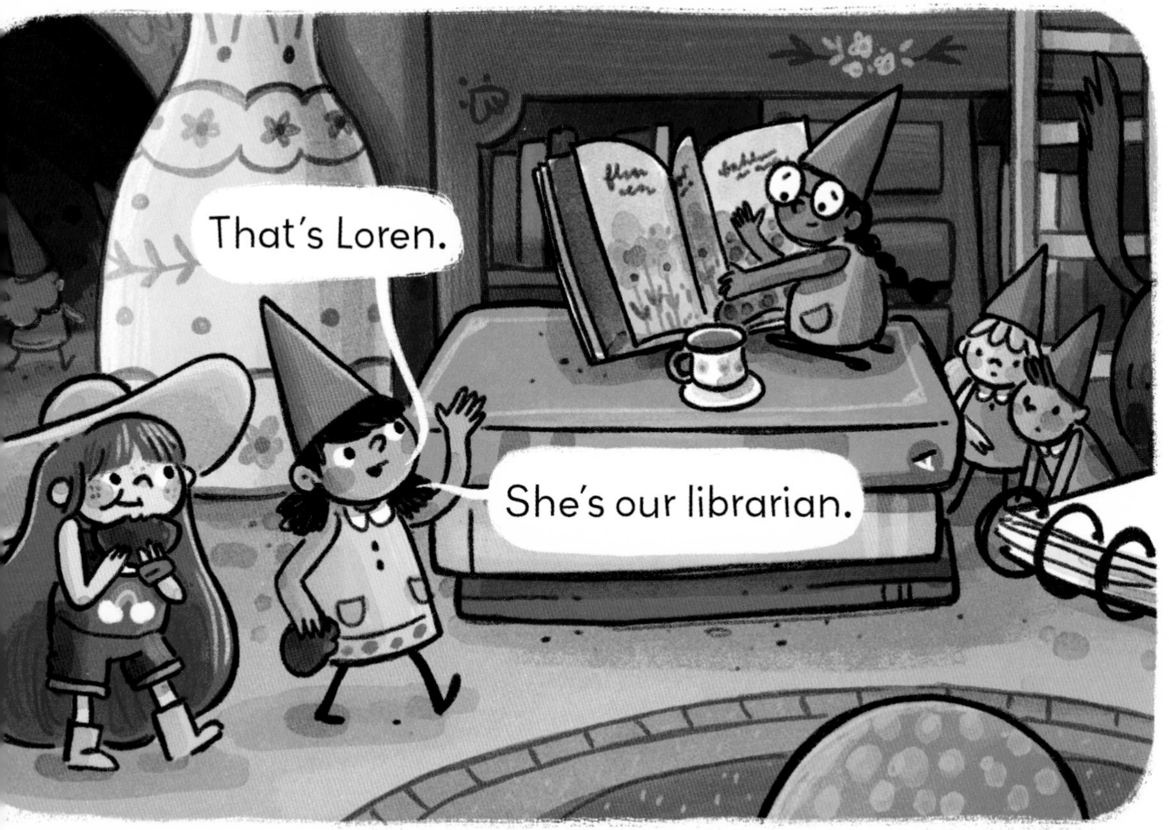
That's Loren.
She's our librarian.

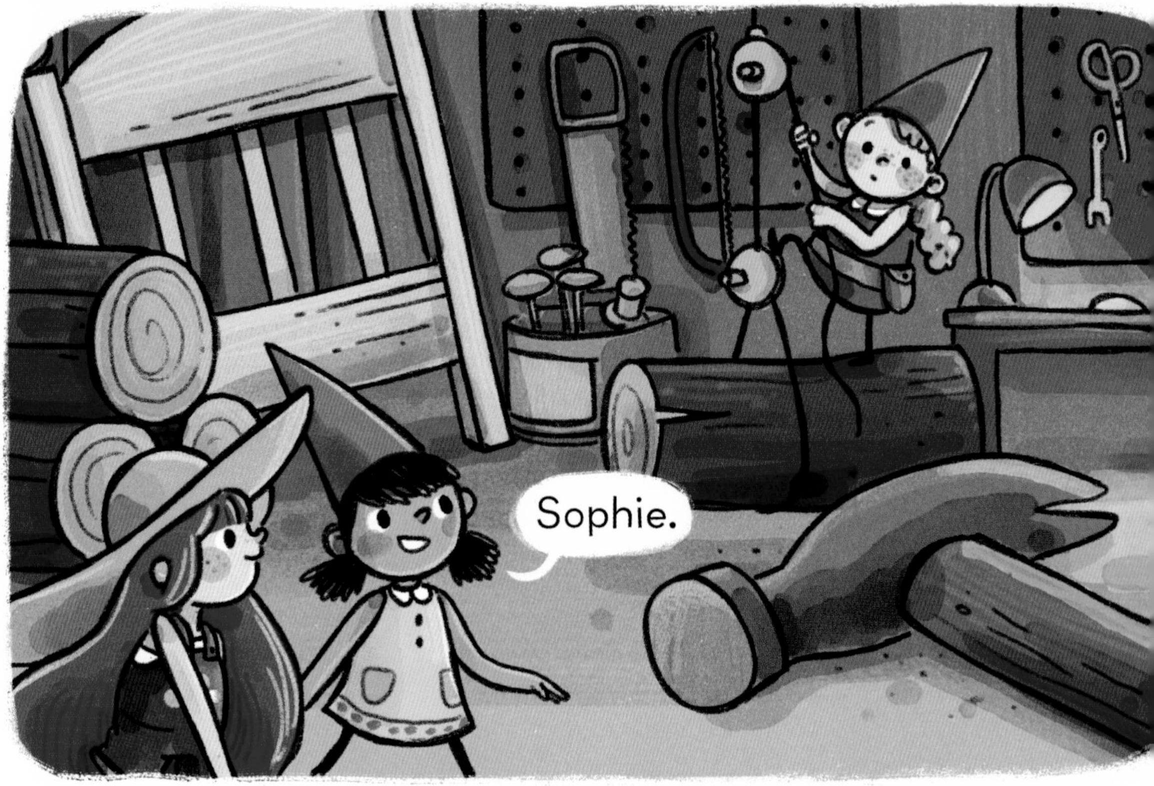
Sophie.

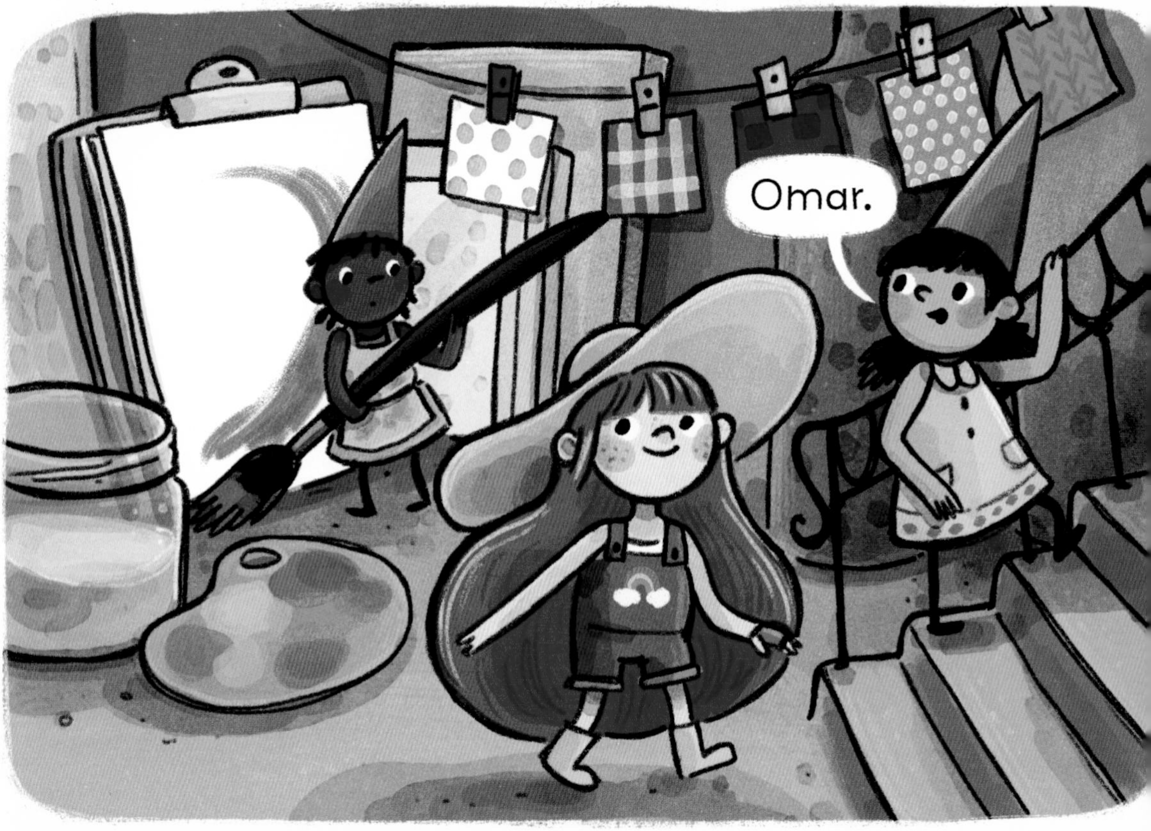
Omar.

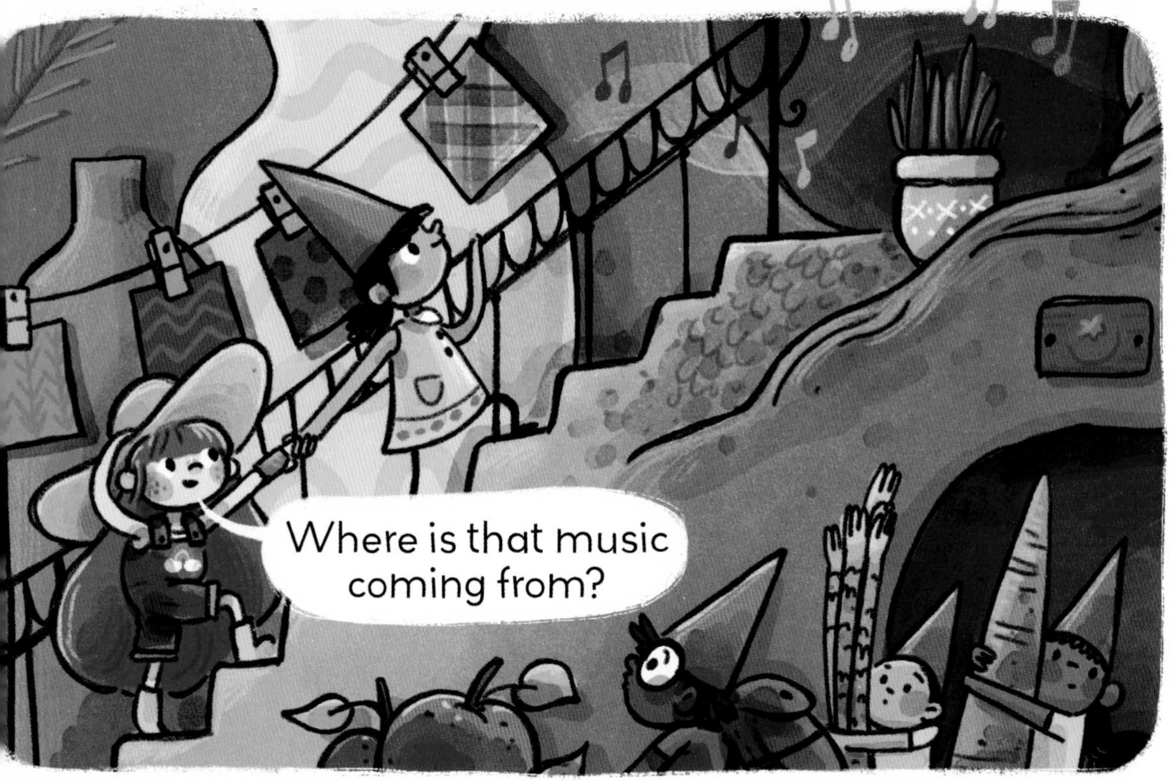
Where is that music coming from?

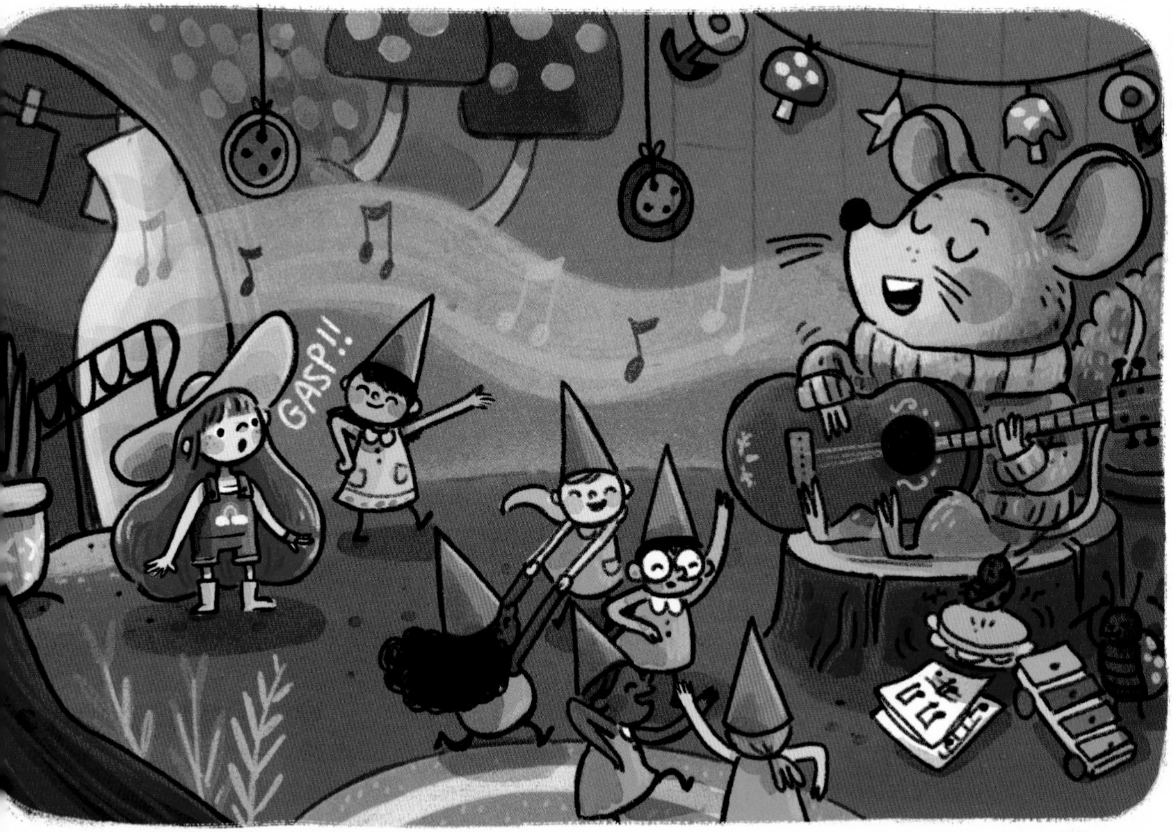
GASP!!

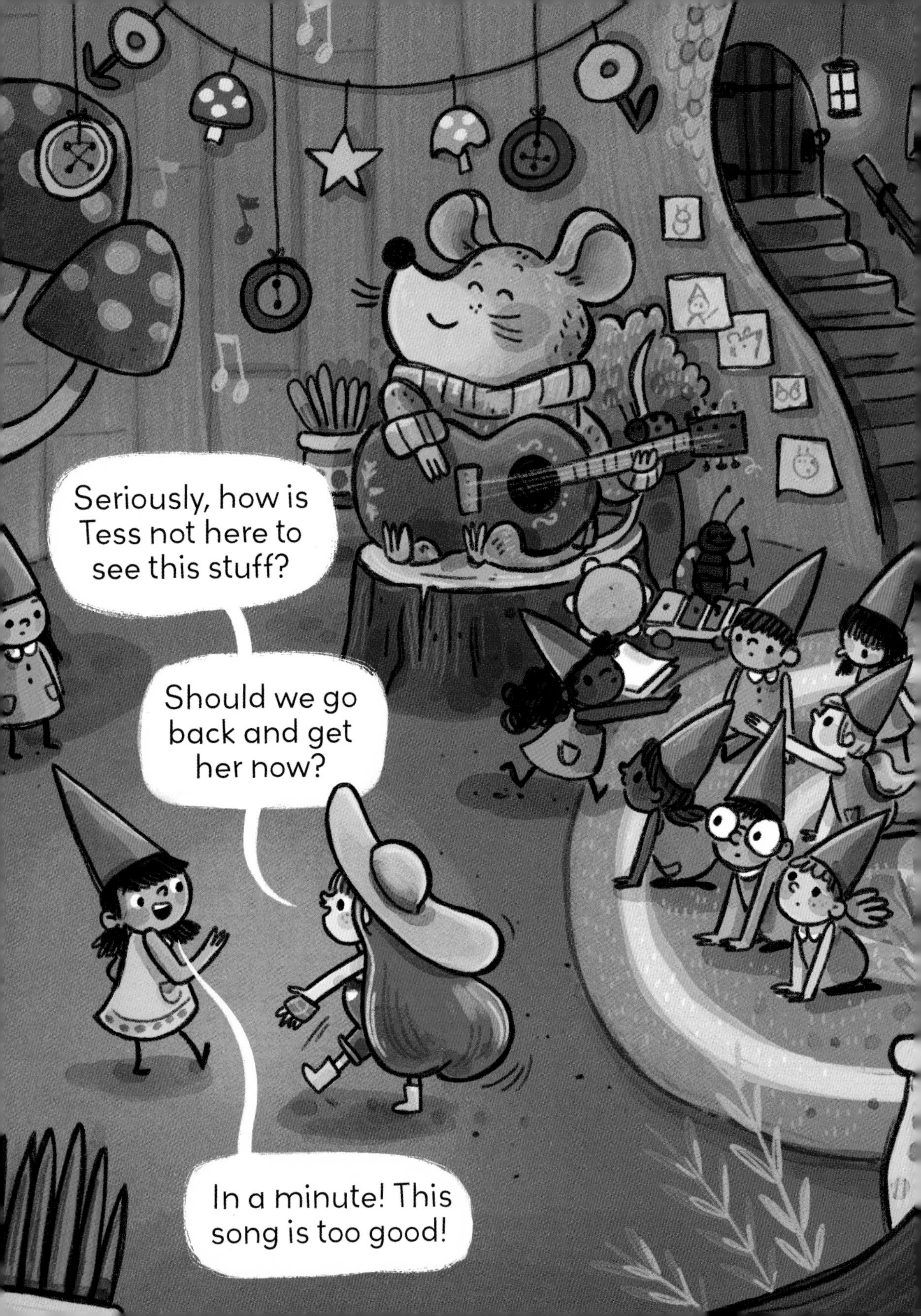
Seriously, how is Tess not here to see this stuff?
Should we go back and get her now?
In a minute! This song is too good!

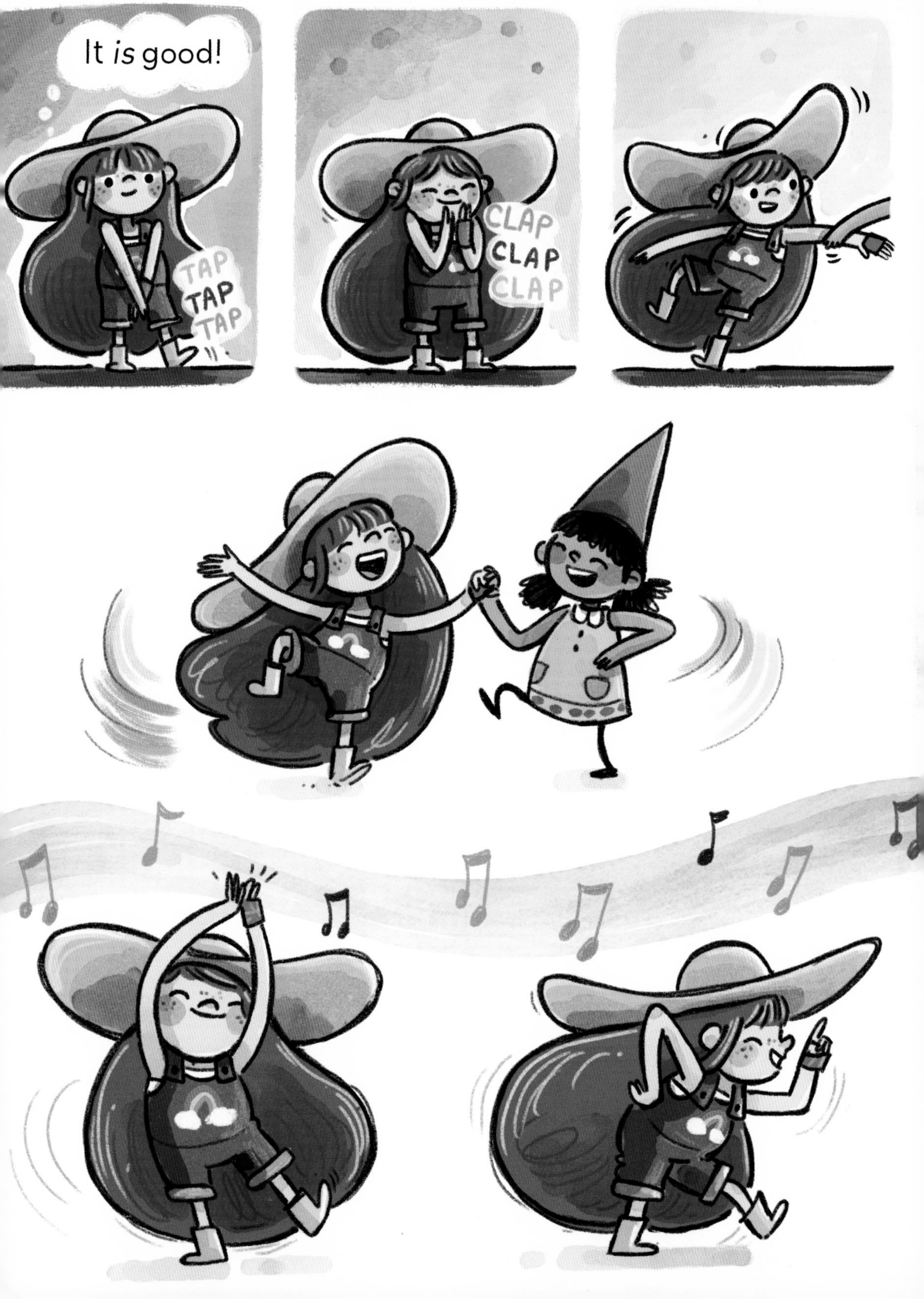
It *is* good!
TAP
TAP
TAP
CLAP
CLAP
CLAP

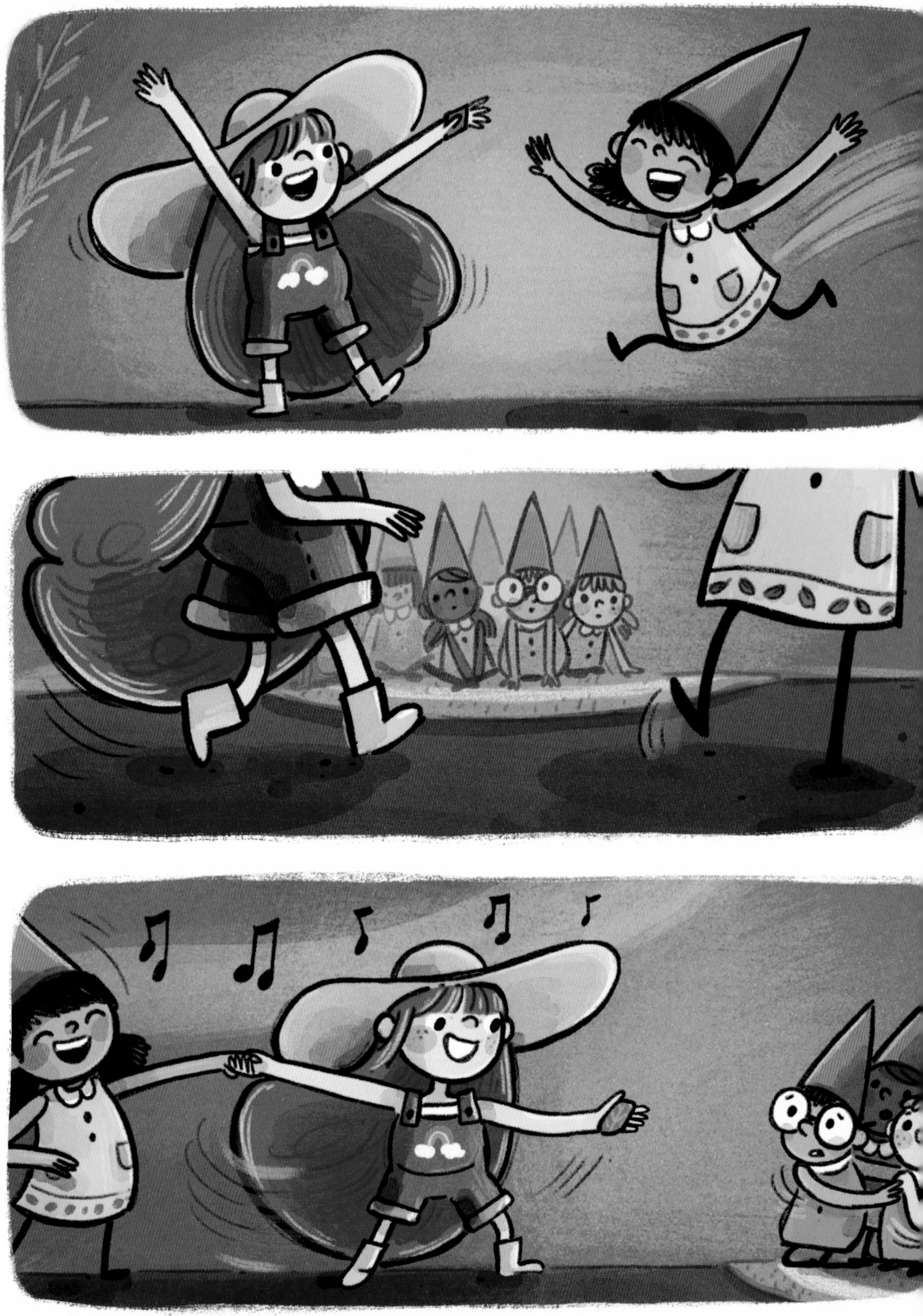

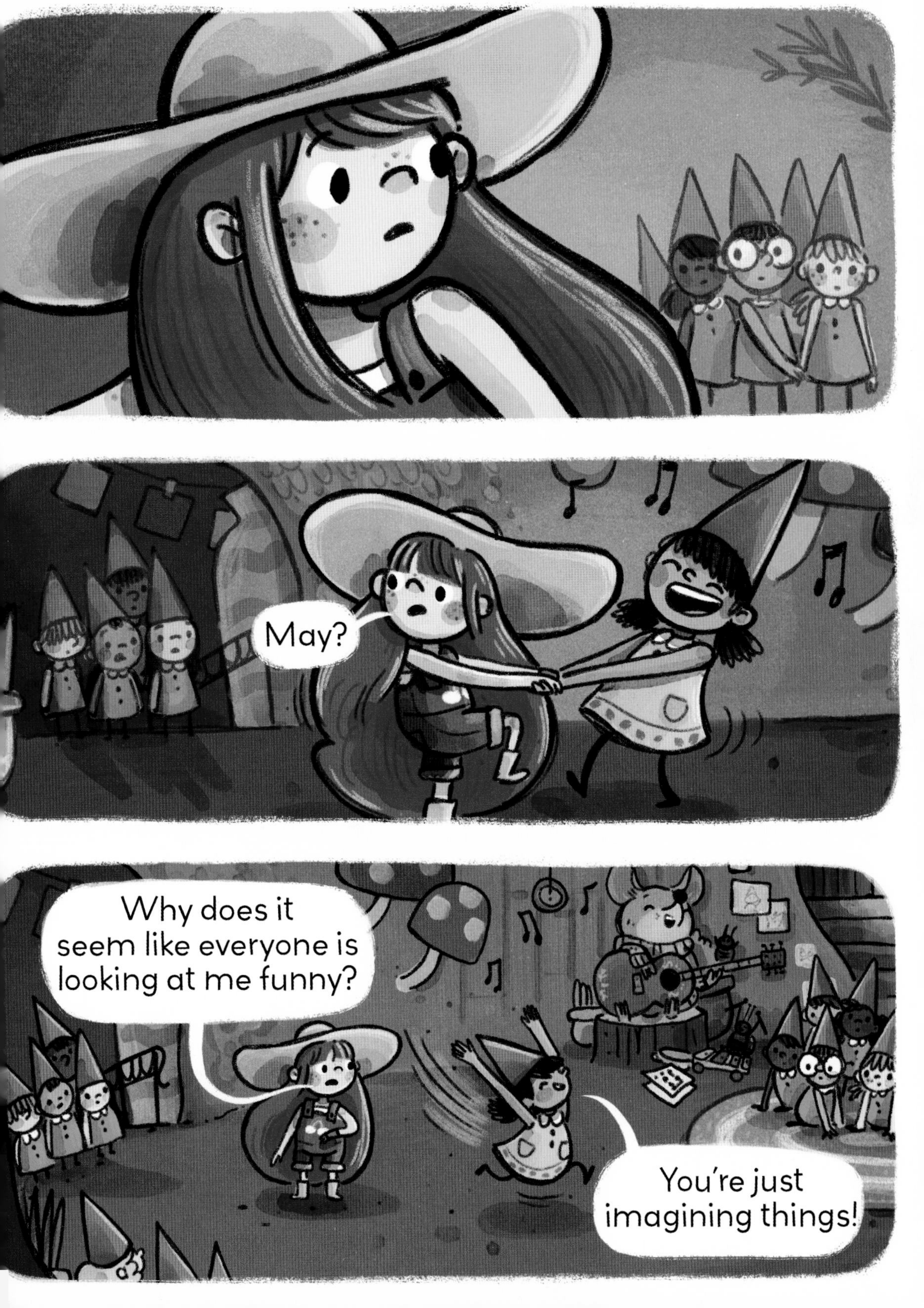
May?
Why does it seem like everyone is looking at me funny?
You're just imagining things!

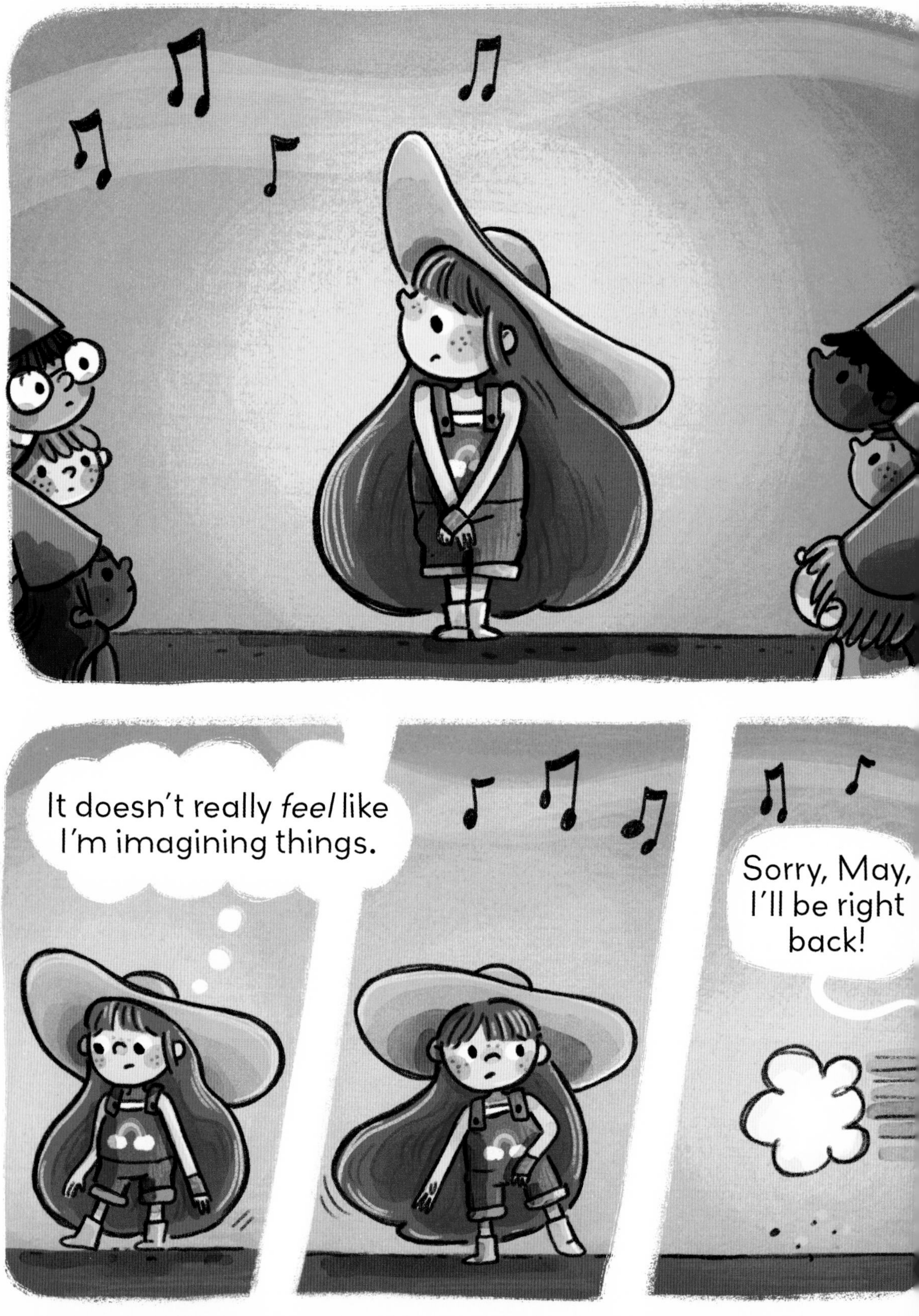
It doesn't really *feel* like I'm imagining things.
Sorry, May, I'll be right back!

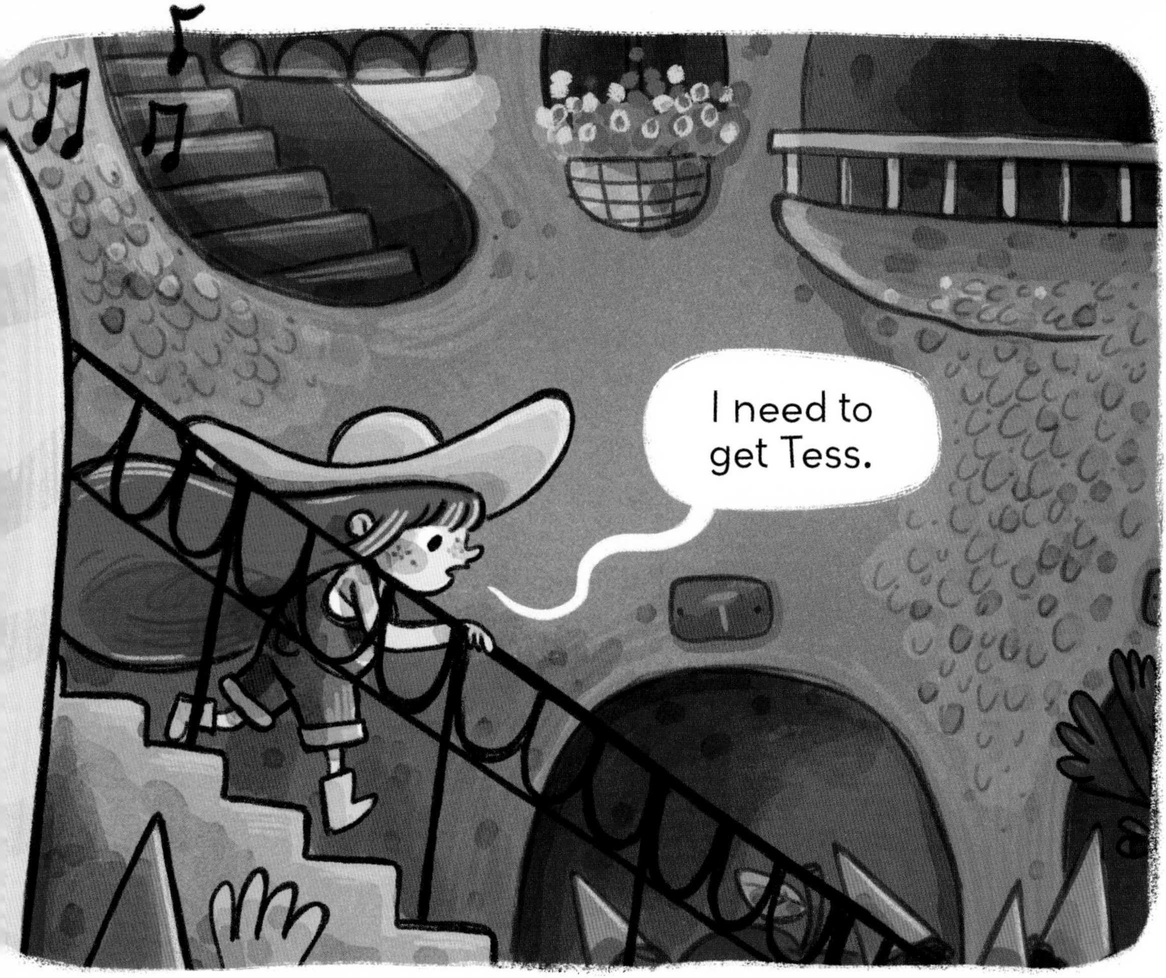
I need to get Tess.

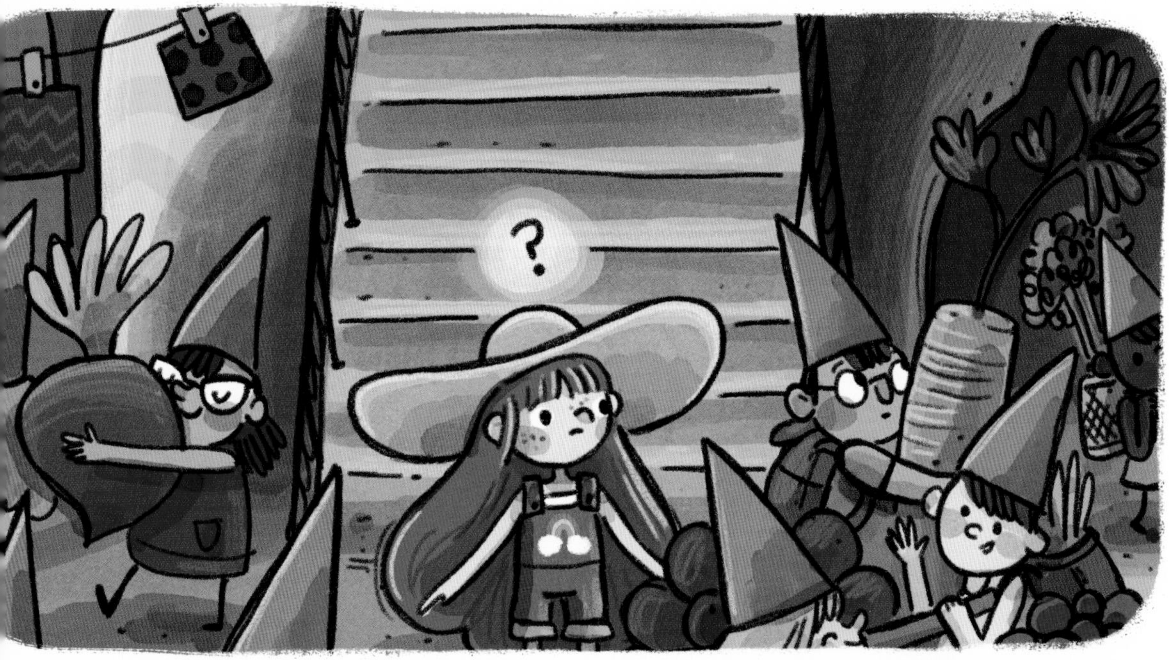
?

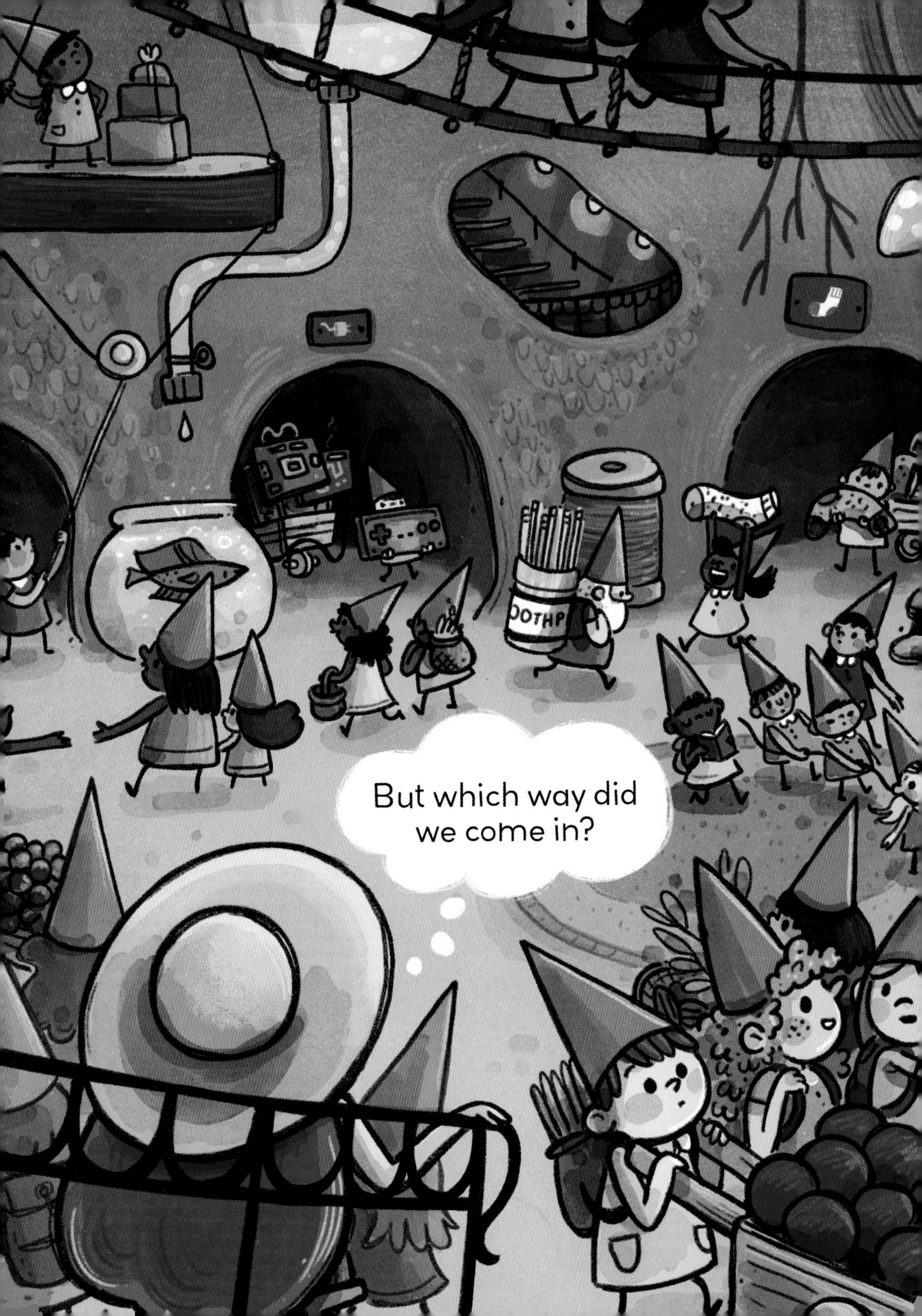
OOTHP
But which way did we come in?

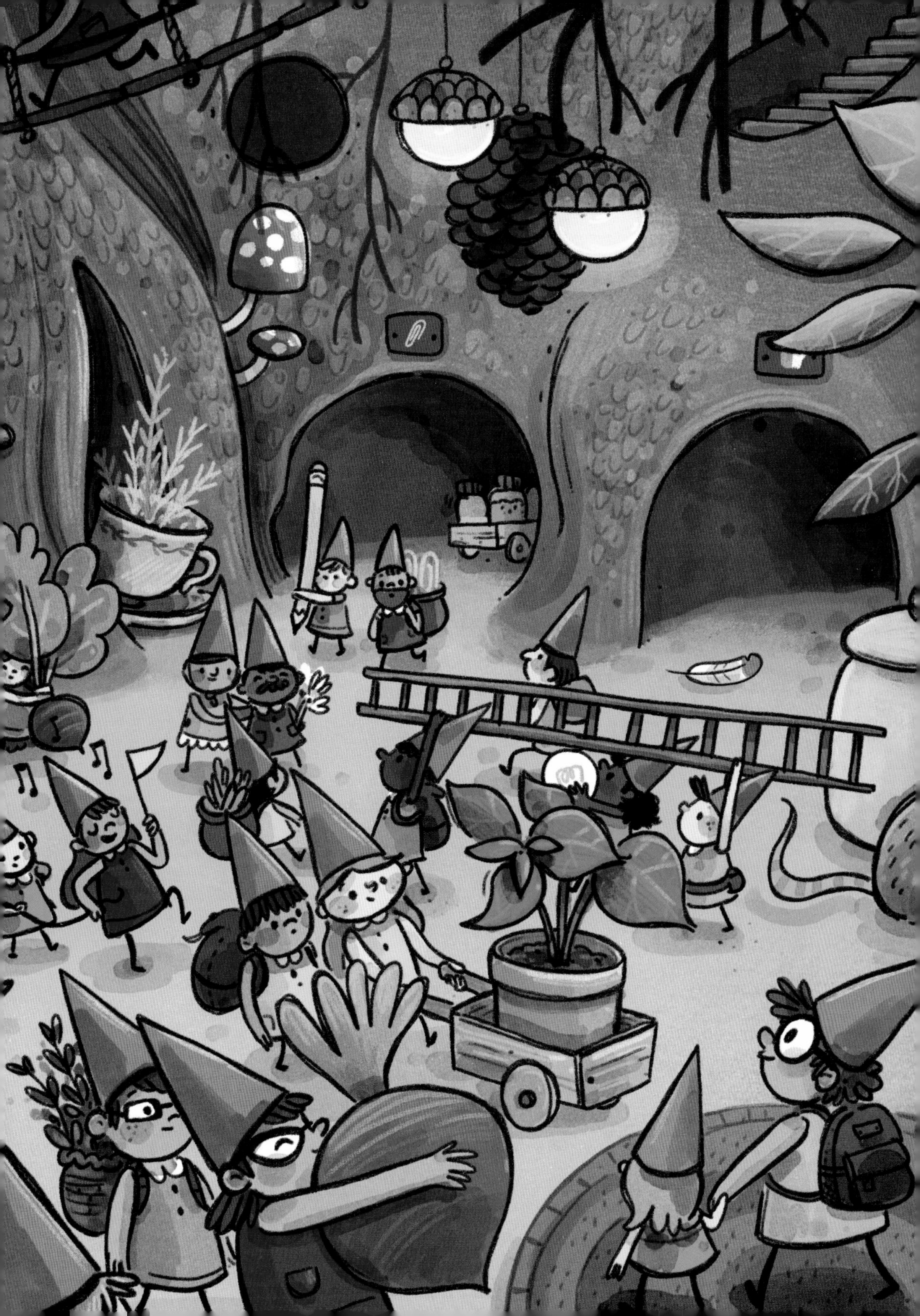

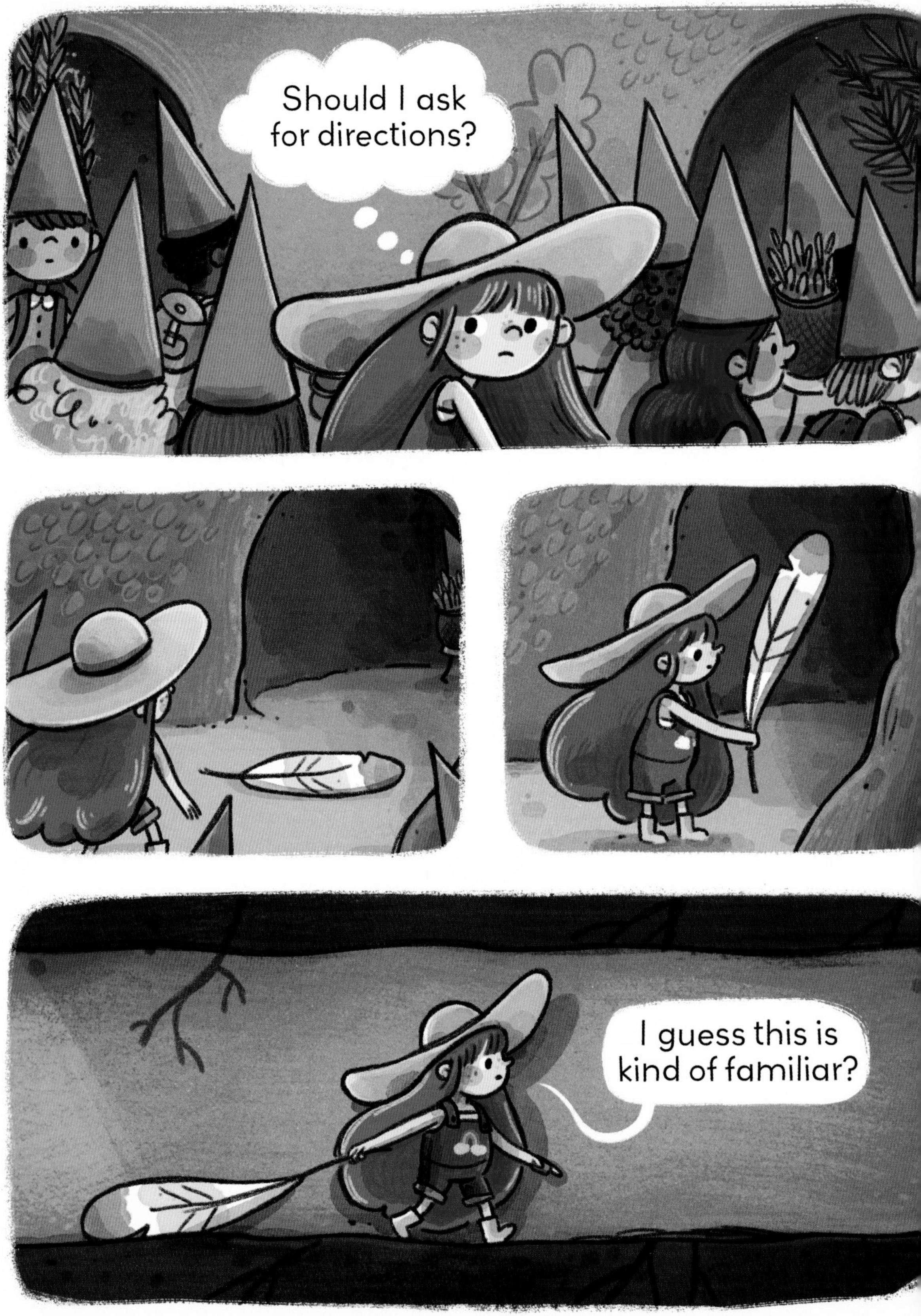
Should I ask for directions?
I guess this is kind of familiar?

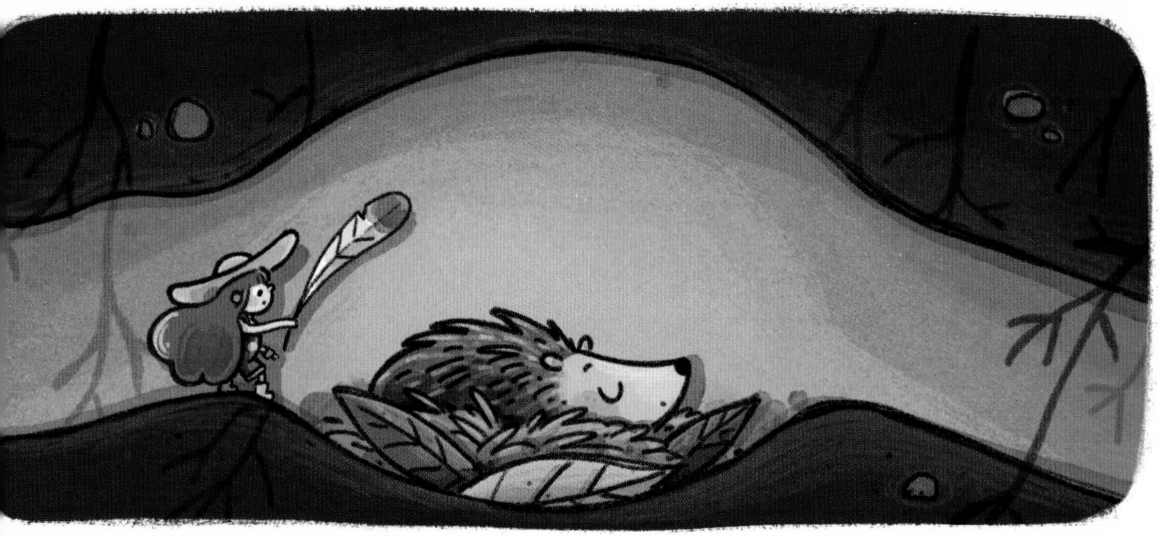

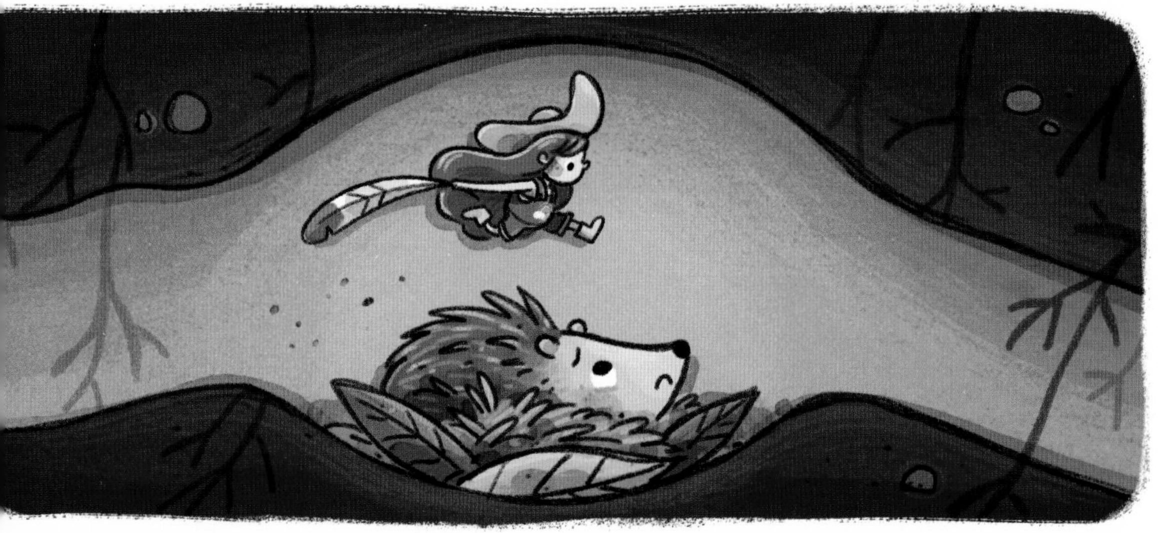

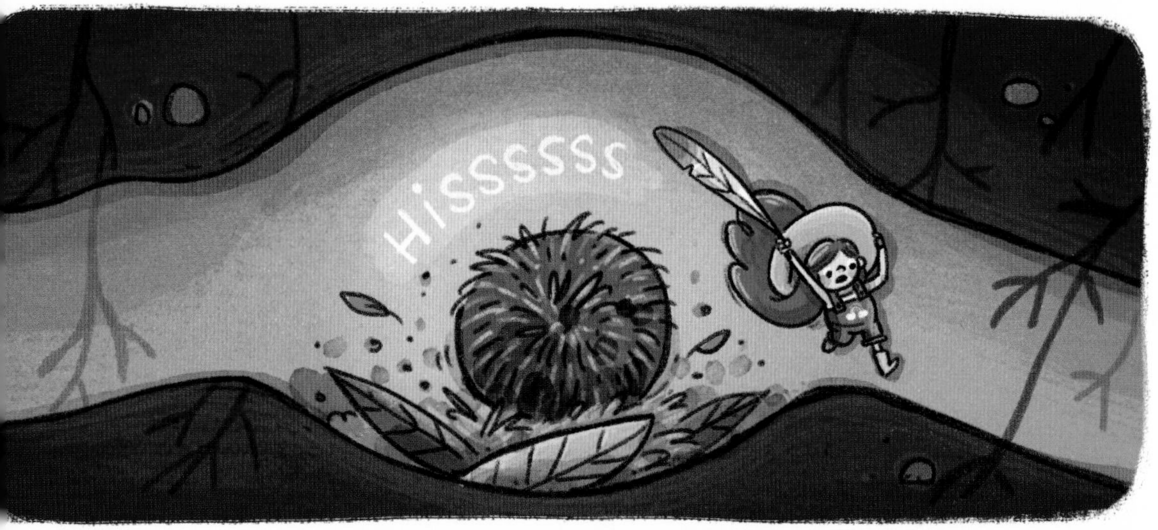
HISSSSSS

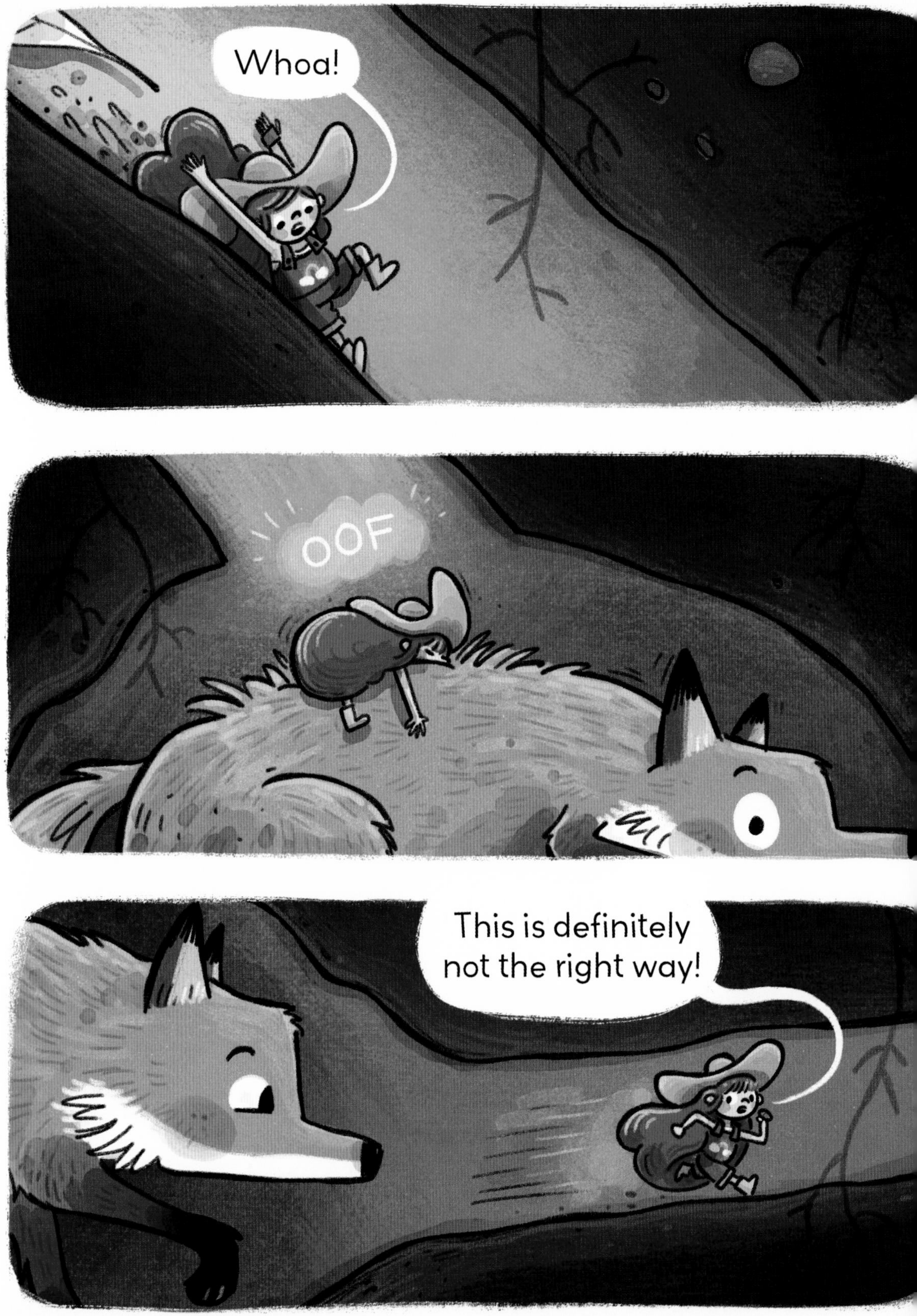
Whoa!
OOF
This is definitely not the right way!

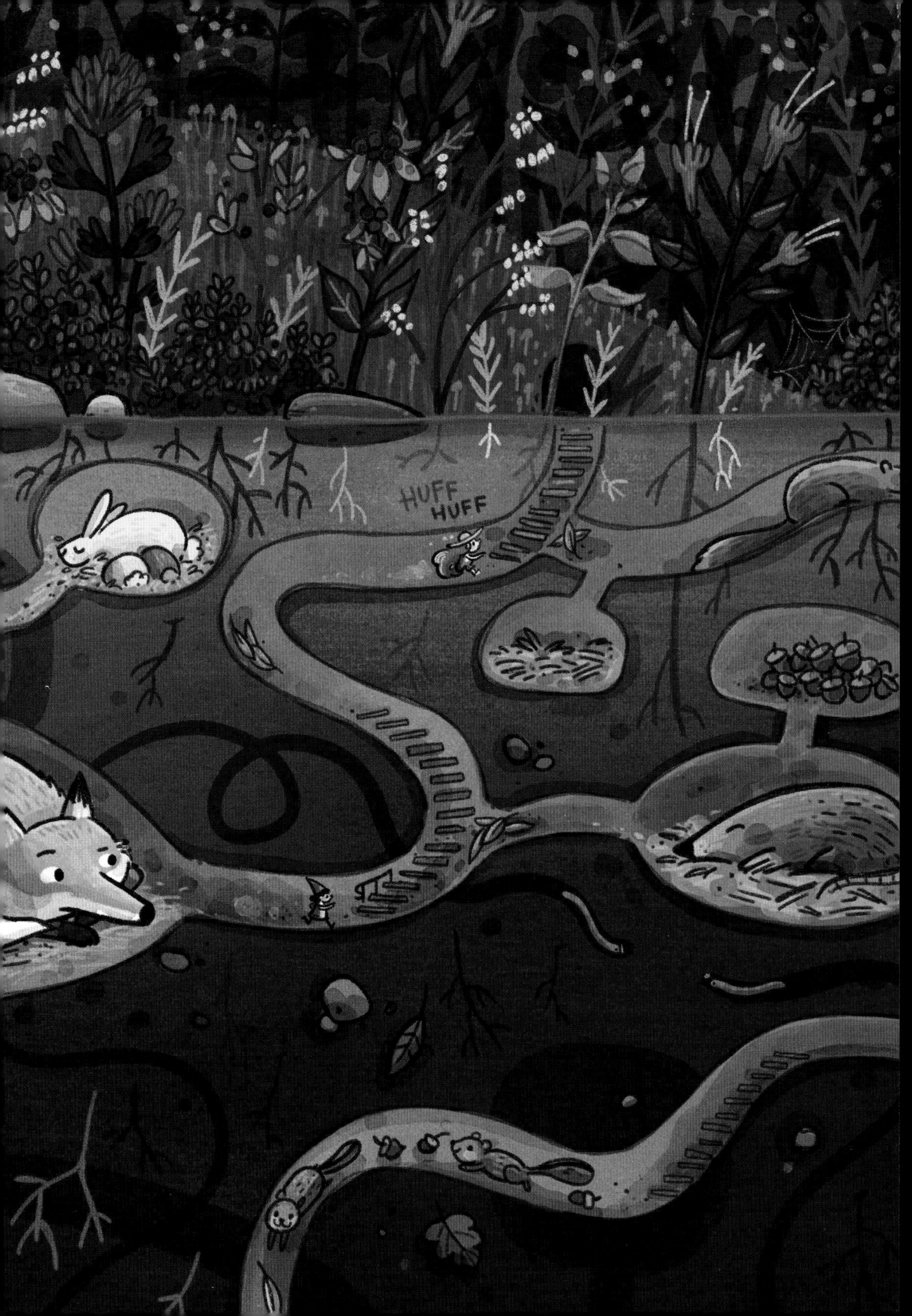
HUFF
HUFF

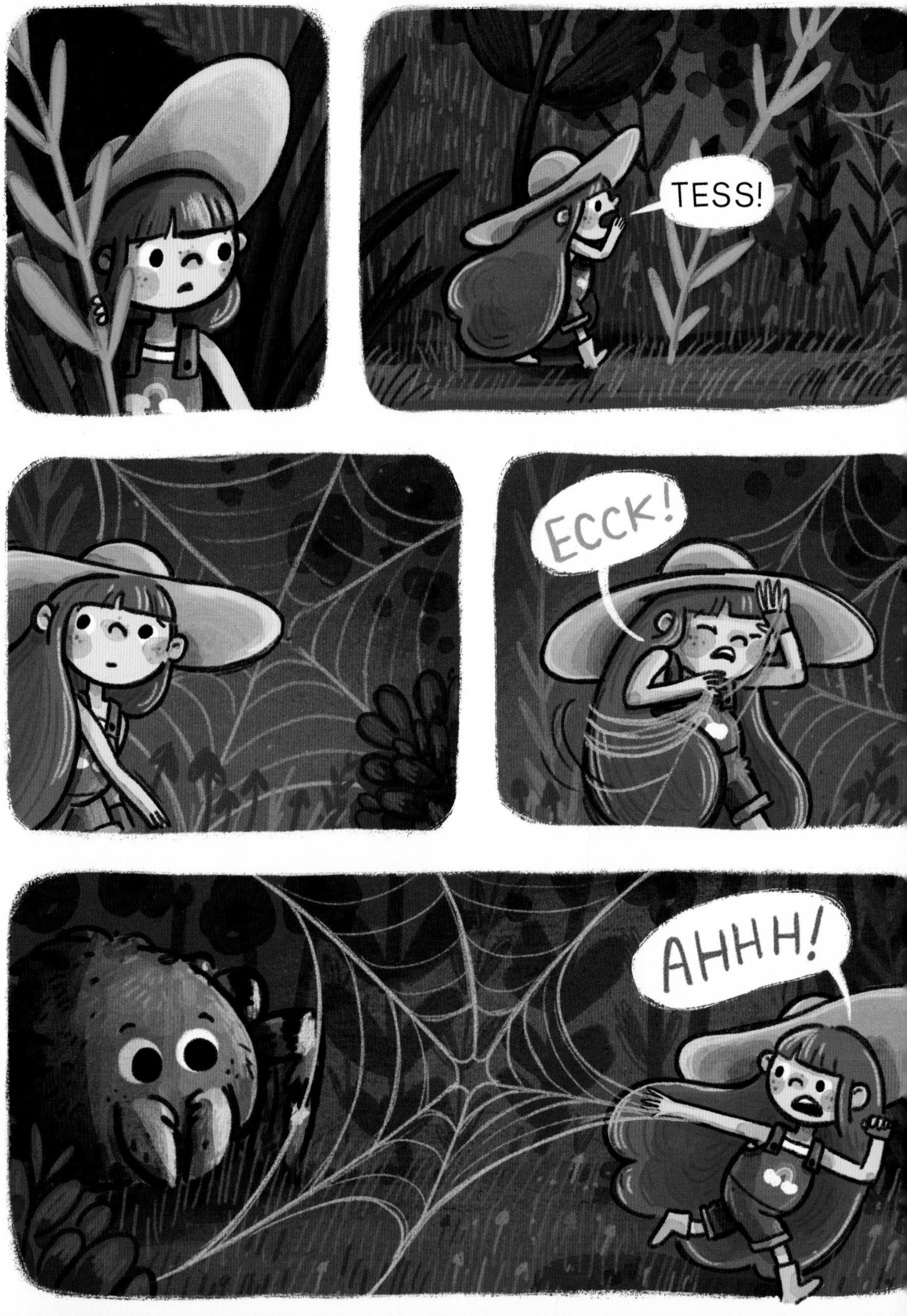
TESS!
ECCK!
AHHH!

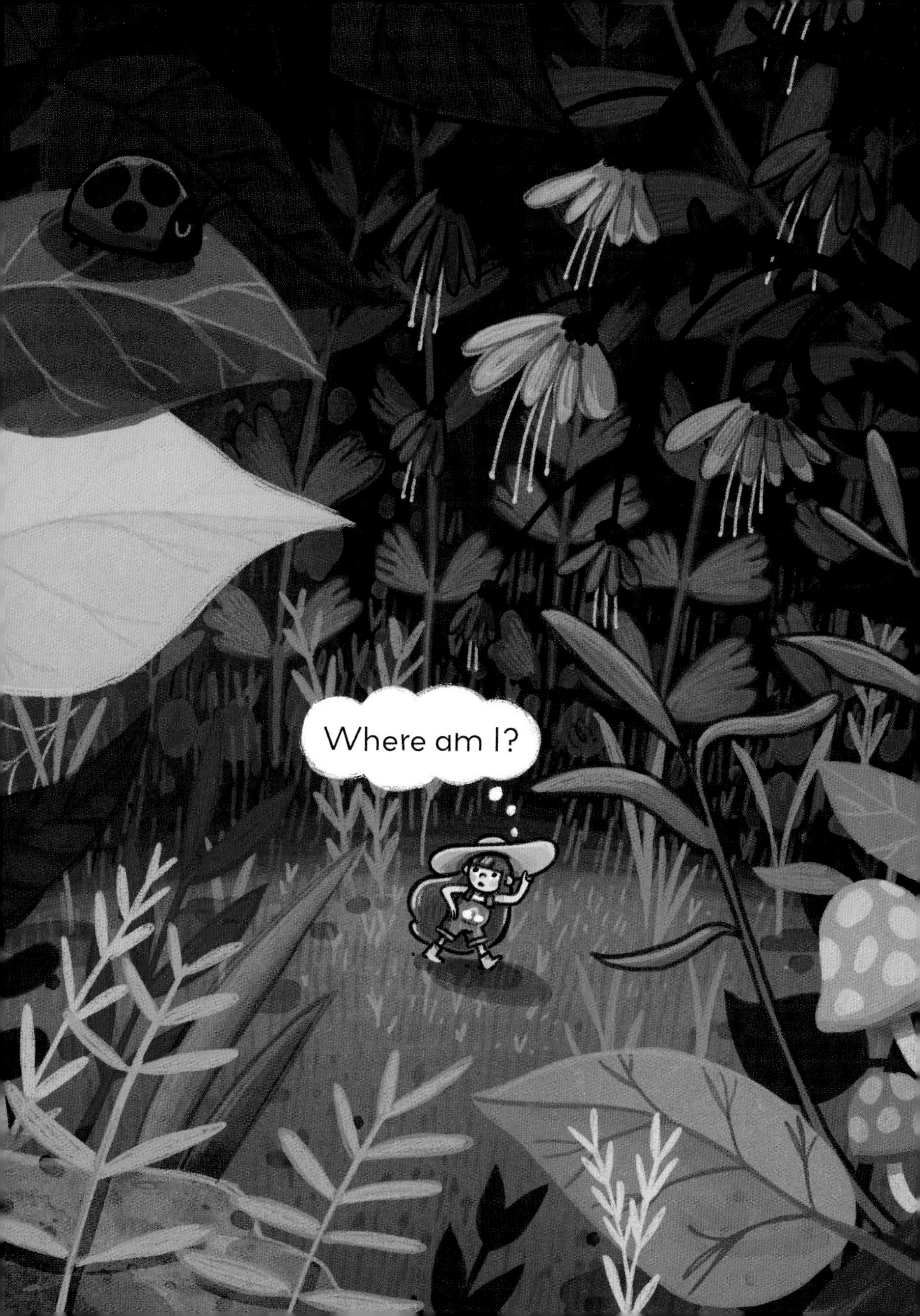
Where am I?

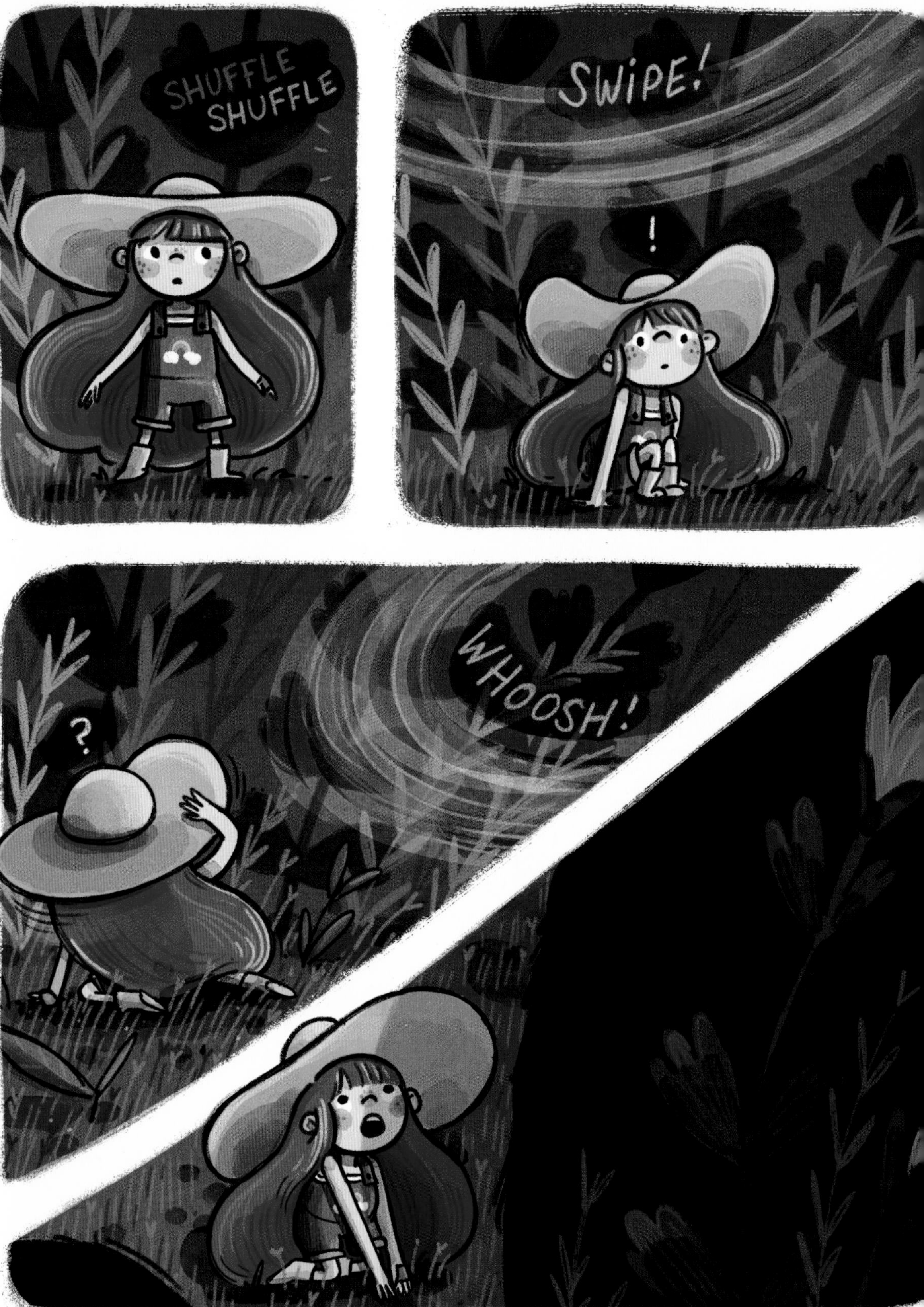
SHUFFLE SHUFFLE
SWIPE!
!
?
WHOOSH!

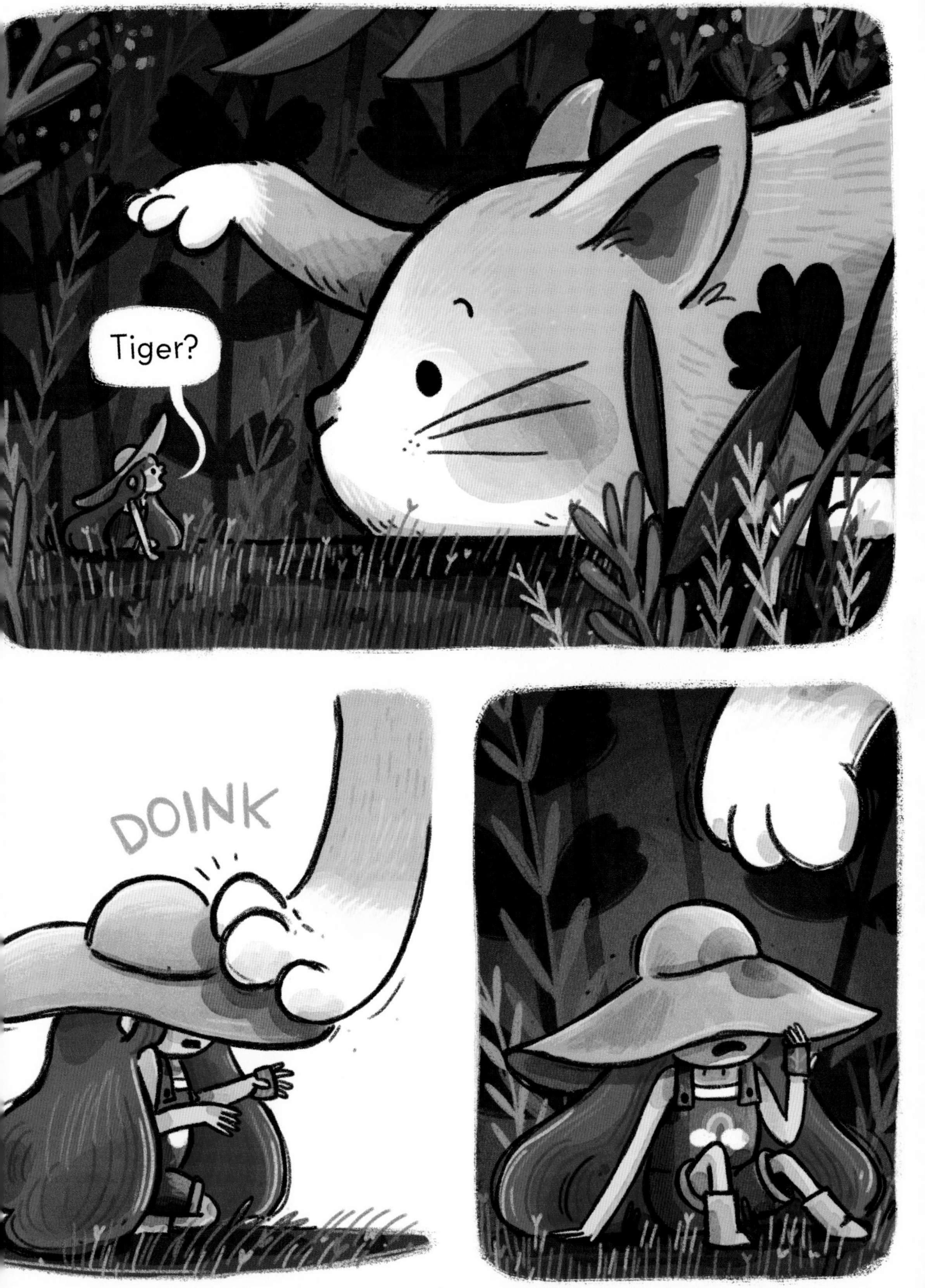
Tiger?
DOINK

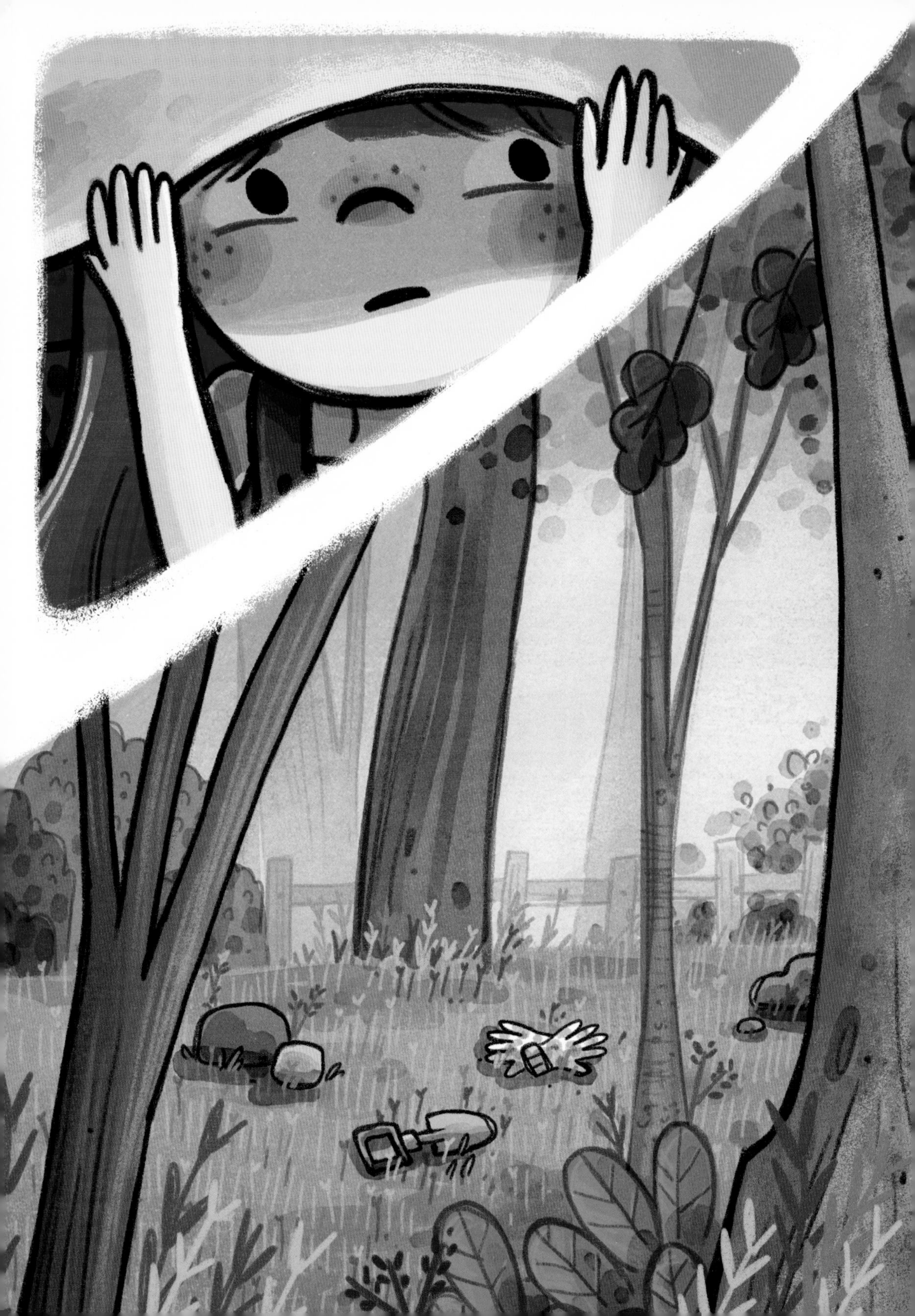

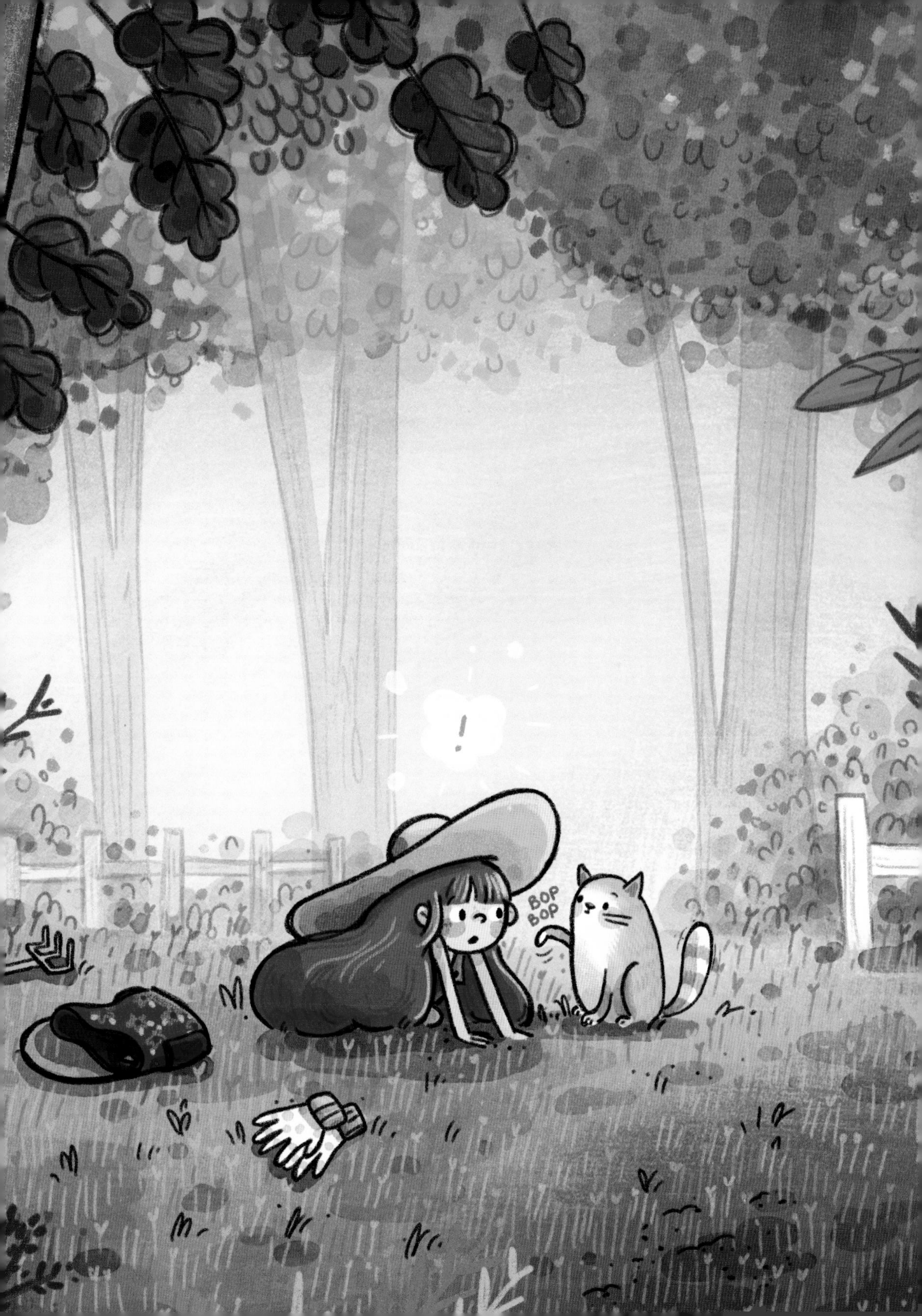
!
BOP
BOP

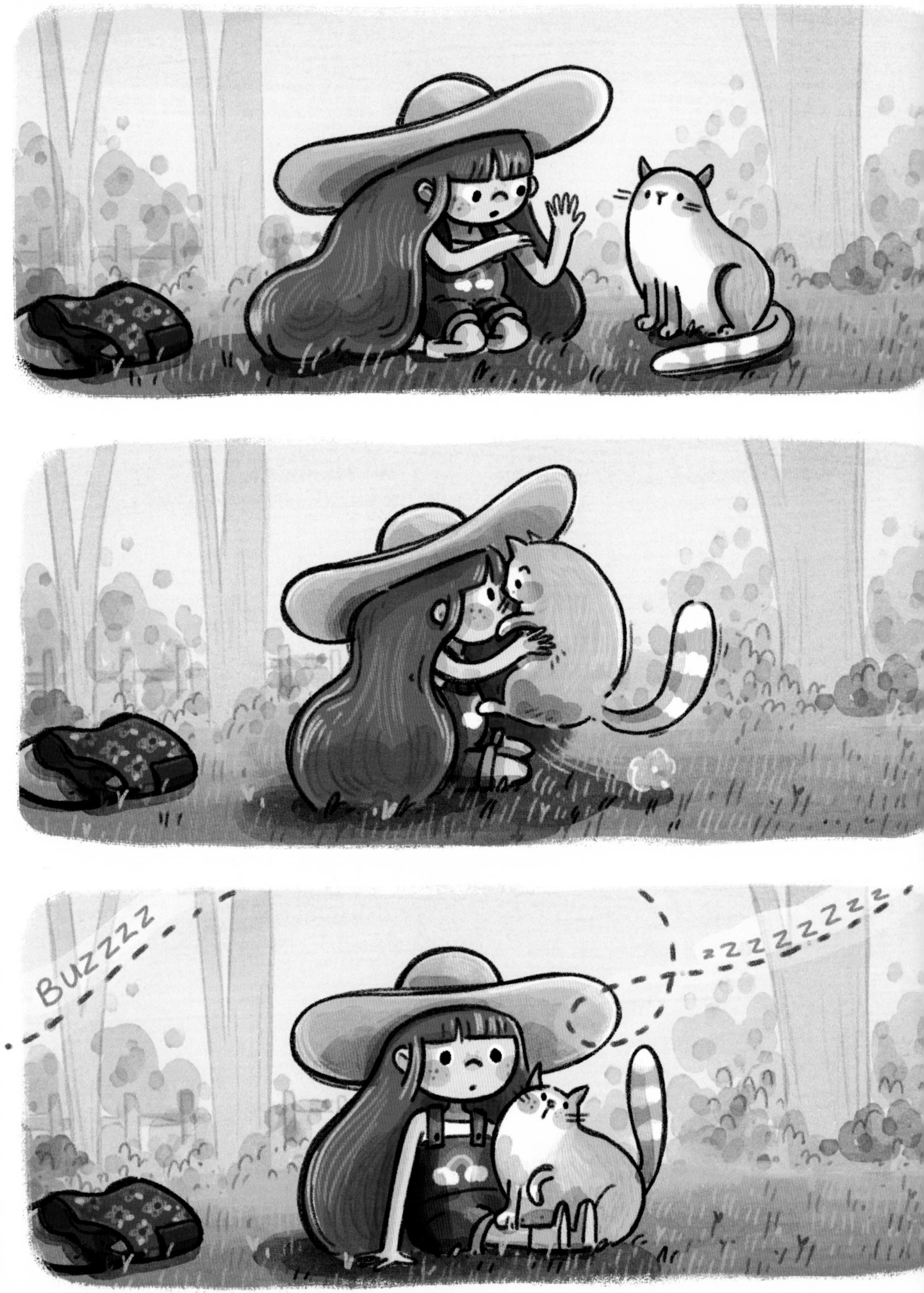
Buzzzz
zzzzzzzzz

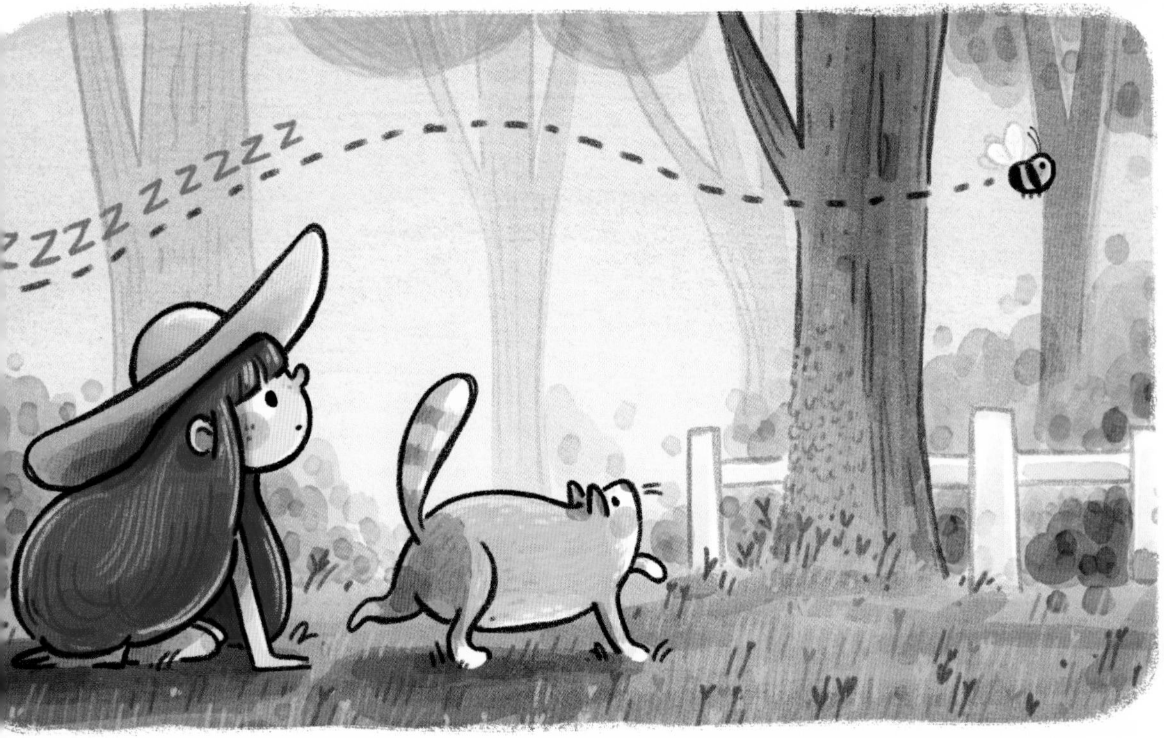
ZZZZZZZZZZZ

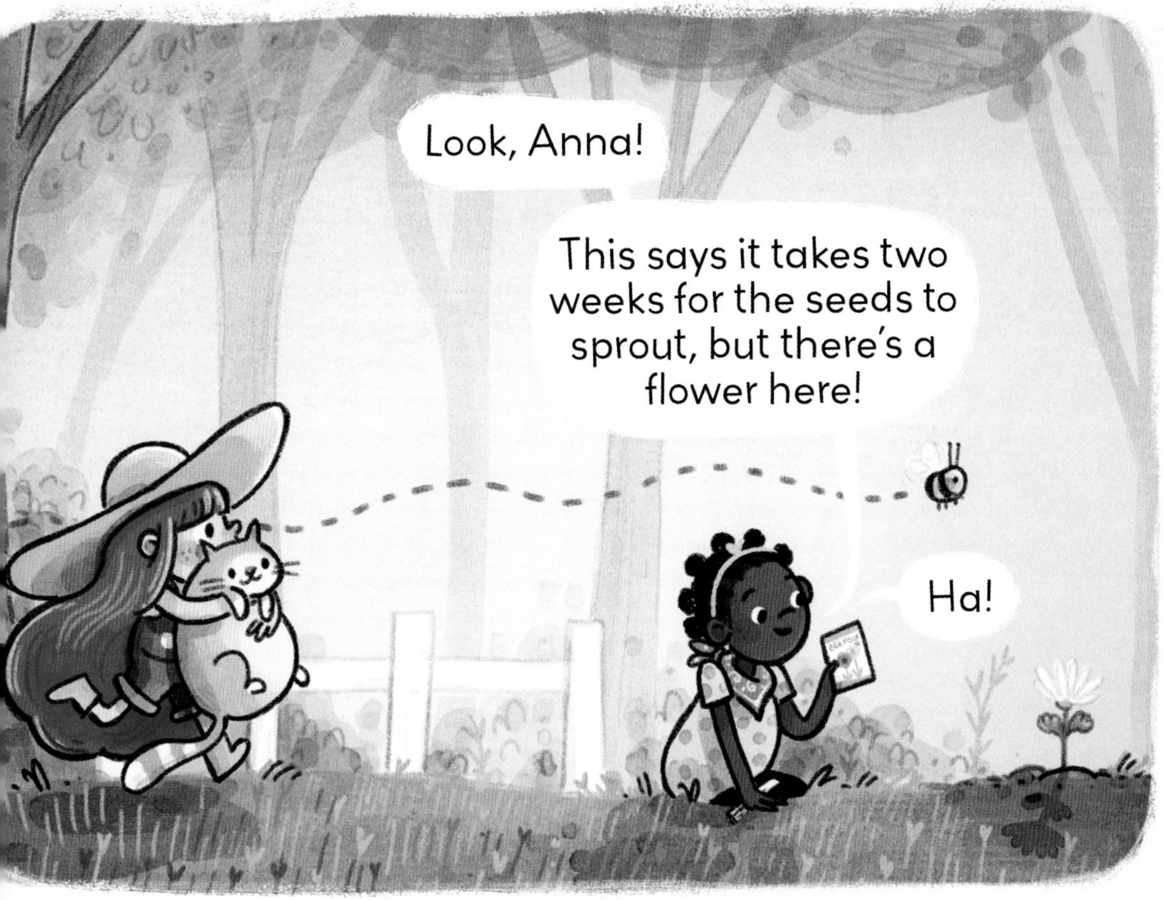
Look, Anna!
This says it takes two weeks for the seeds to sprout, but there's a flower here!
Ha!

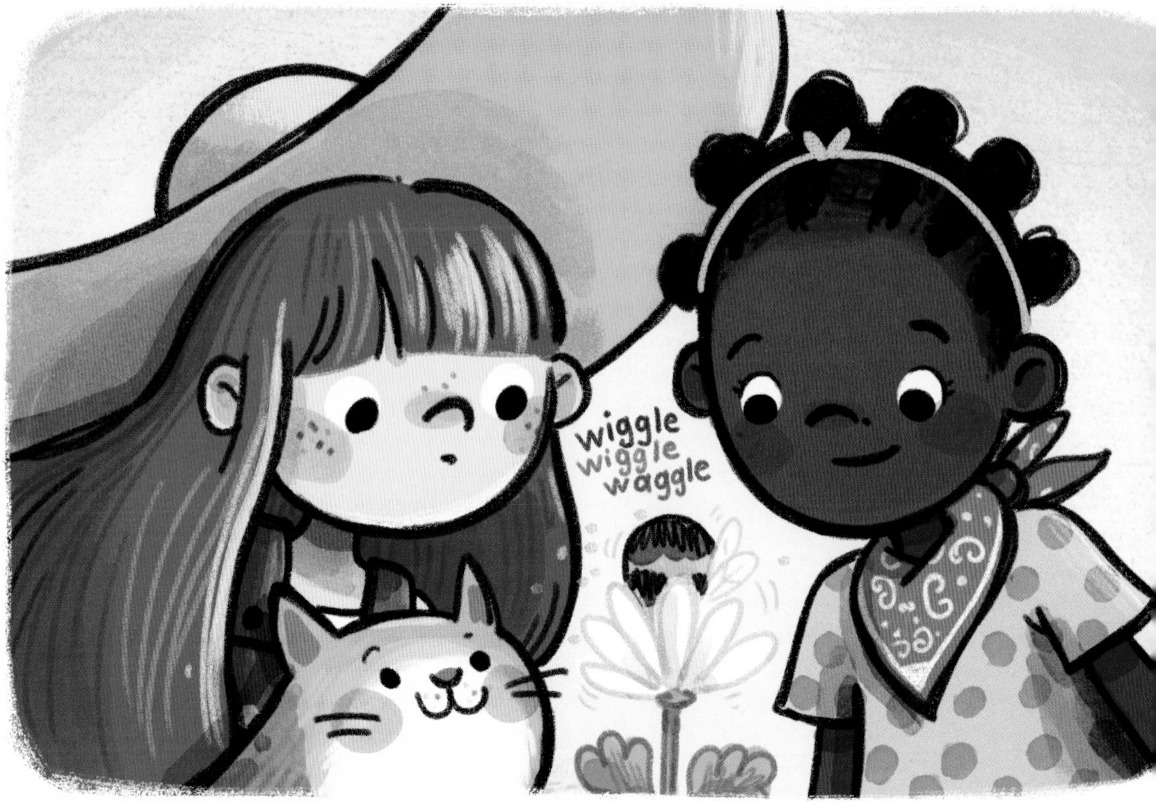
wiggle
wiggle
waggle

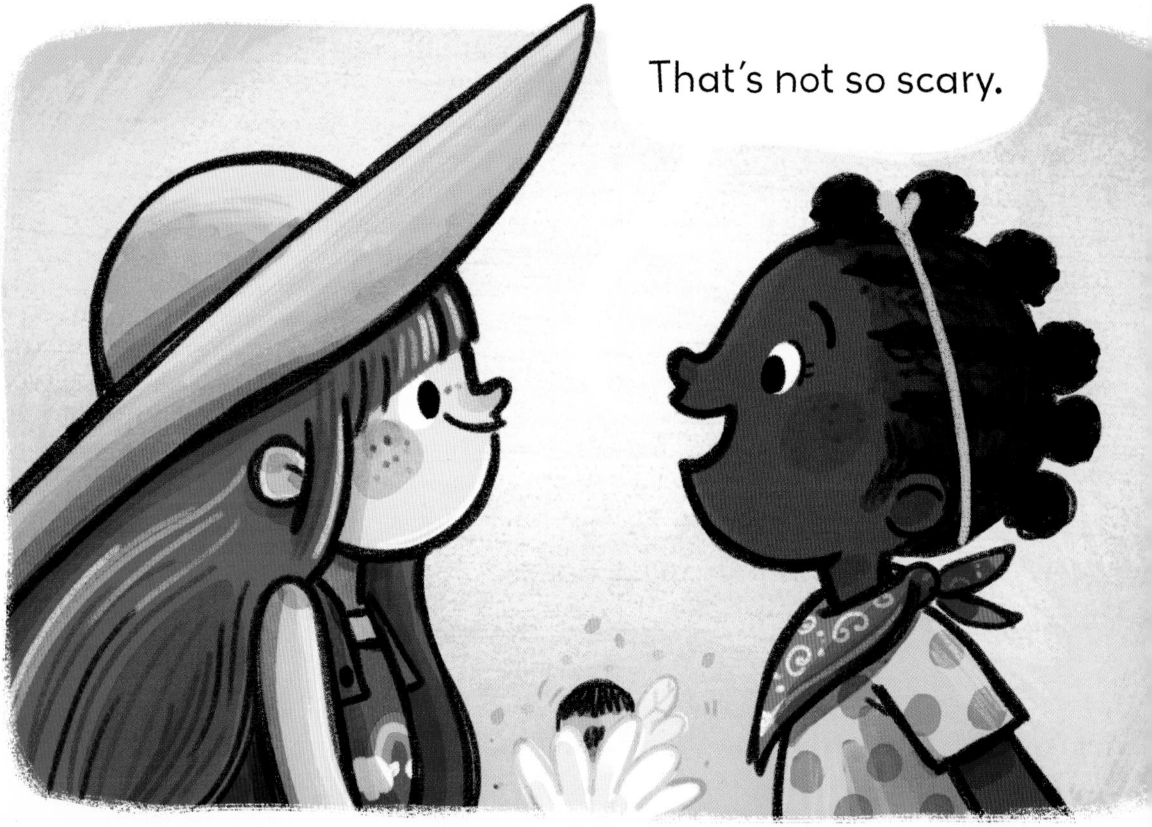
That's not so scary.

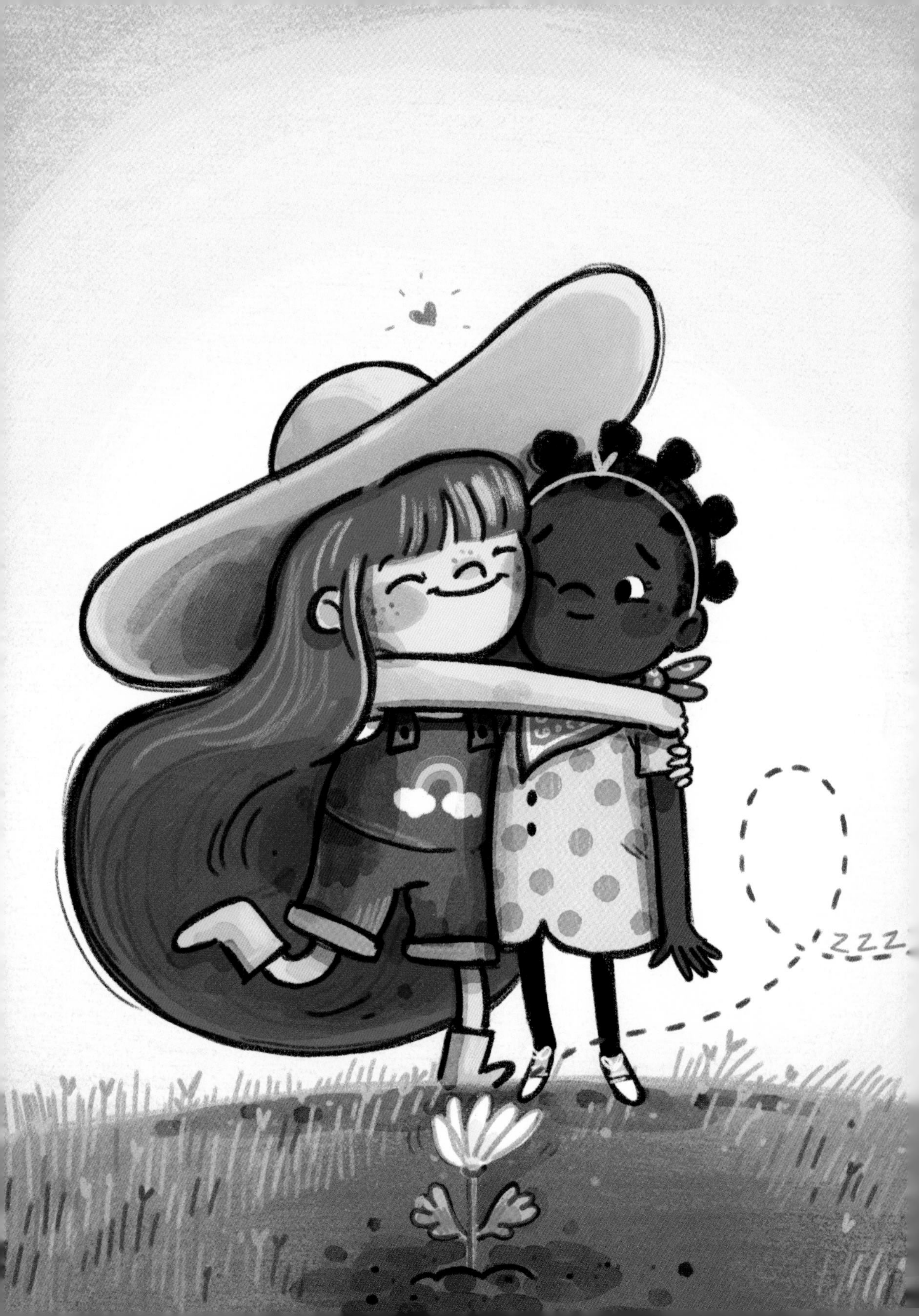
ZZZ

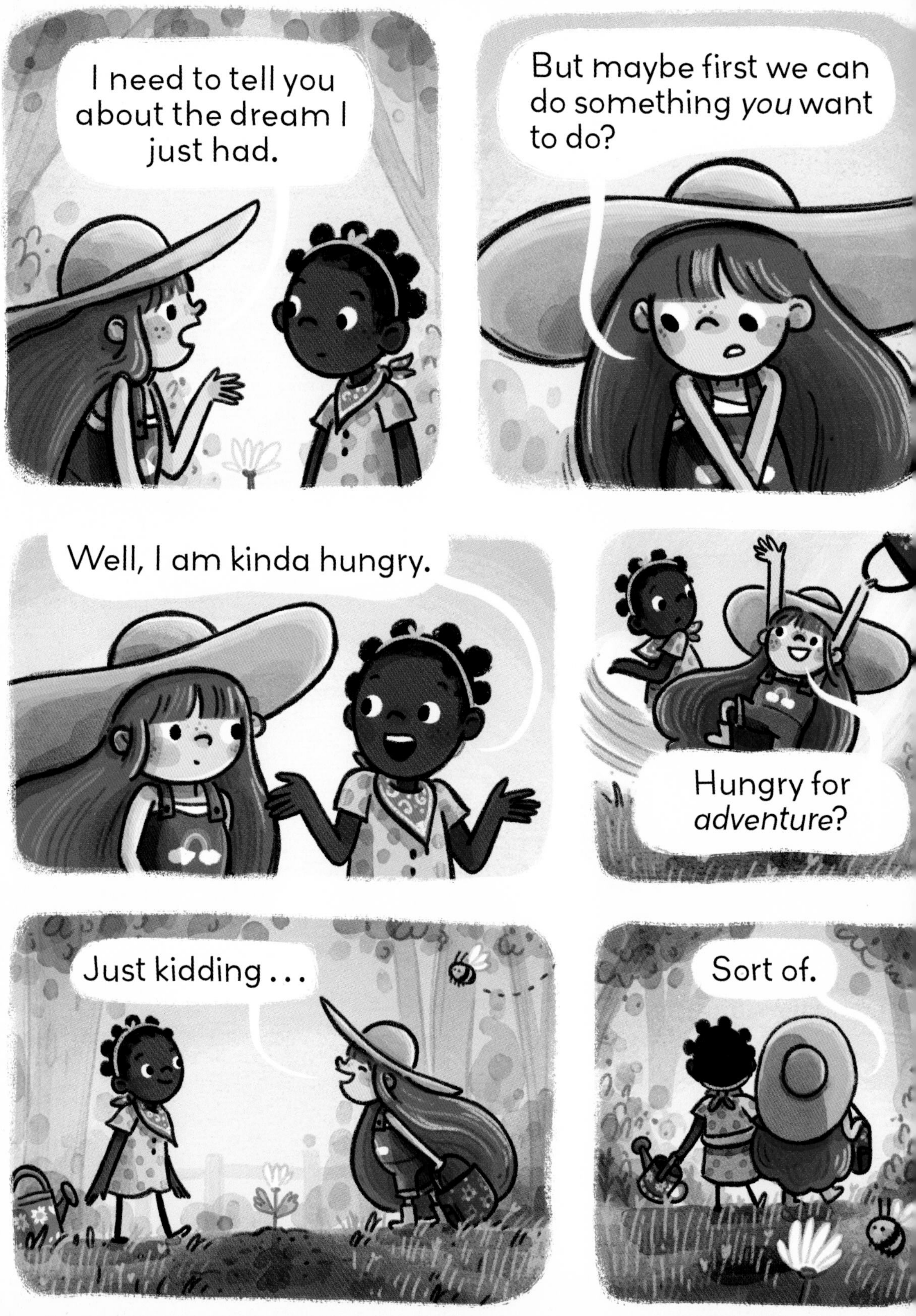
I need to tell you about the dream I just had.
But maybe first we can do something *you* want to do?
Well, I am kinda hungry.
Hungry for *adventure*?
Just kidding . . .
Sort of.

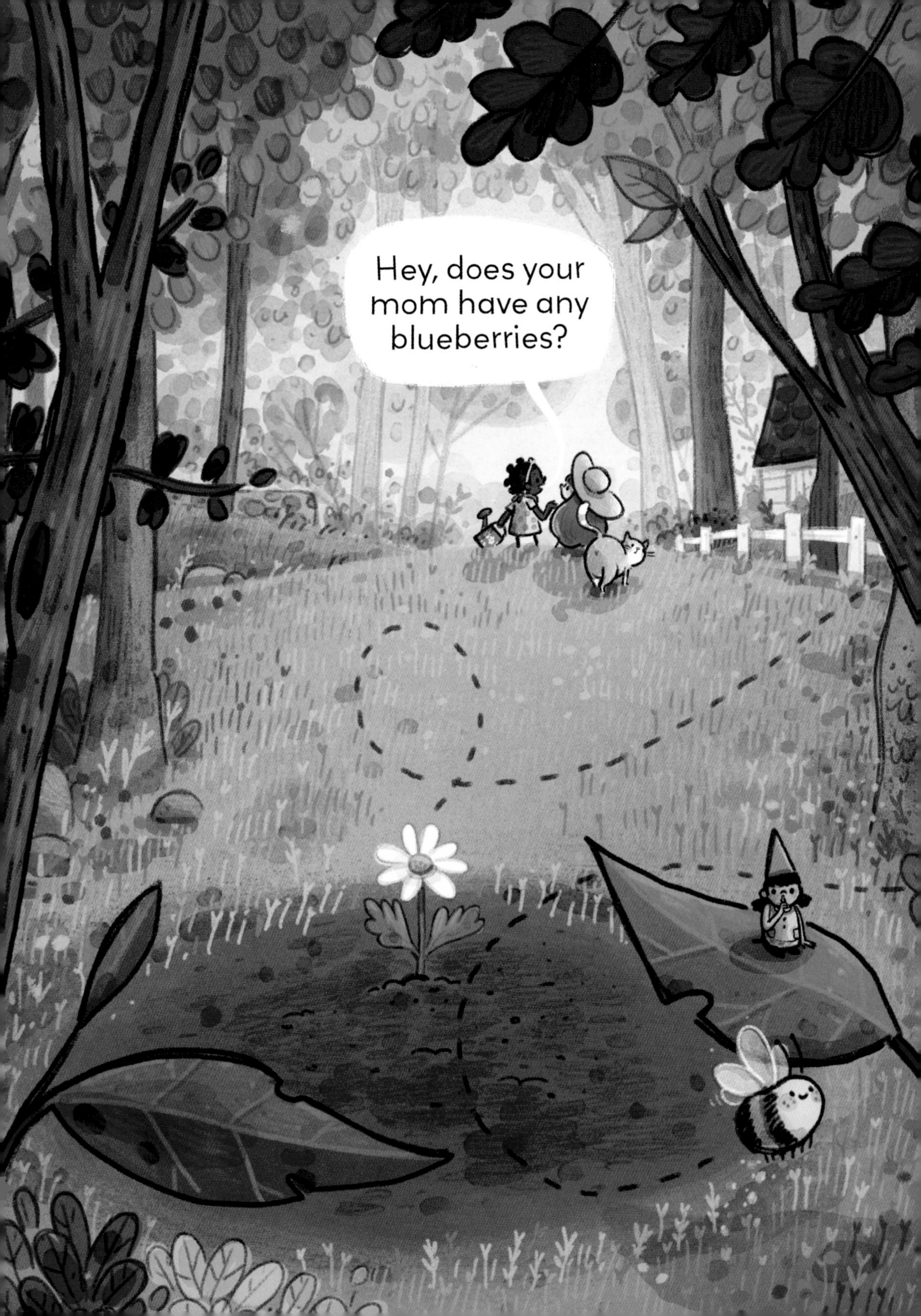
Hey, does your mom have any blueberries?

For Mom and Dad

Library of Congress Control Number 2021942300
ISBN 978-1-4197-5020-5

Text and illustrations copyright © 2022 Renée Kurilla
Book design by Pamela Notarantonio

Printed and bound in China
10 9 8 7 6 5 4 3 2 1

Amulet Books are available at special discounts when purchased in quantity for premiums and promotions as well as fundraising or educational use. Special editions can also be created to specification. For details, contact specialsales@abramsbooks.com or the address below.

Amulet Books® is a registered trademark of Harry N. Abrams, Inc.

ABRAMS The Art of Books
195 Broadway, New York, NY 10007
abramsbooks.com